D1571033

Bleeding Chaos

A LOVE & LYRICS NOVEL

USA TODAY BESTSELLING AUTHOR

NIKKI ASH

One day at a time...

Author's Note

Like real life, the characters in Bleeding Chaos are far from perfect, make morally gray decisions, and deal with subjects that may be sensitive for some readers. If you are looking for a safe romance, this story is not for you. Trigger warnings (which contain spoilers) can be found on my website: Love & Lyrics Trigger Warnings.

Playlist

"The Bones"- Maren Morris
"All of Me"- John Legend
"Too Good at Goodbyes"- Sam Smith
"Love The Way You Lie"- Eminem feat. Rihanna
"Whatcha Say"- Jason Derulo
"Don't Let Me Down"- The Chainsmokers
"Leave Before You Love Me"- Jonas Brothers and Marshmello
"Without Me"- Halsey
"You Should Be Sad"- Halsey
"Breakeven"- The Script
"Sorry"- Justin Bieber
"Arcade"- Duncan Lawrence
"Memory"- Kane Brown x Black Bear
"Too Much to Ask"-Niall Horan
"Ghost"- Justin Bieber

Someone like me doesn't deserve her time
But that doesn't stop me from wanting to take what's mine
From wanting her heart to be mine
Her body, her soul, all mine
- Gage, Raging Chaos

Prologue

Gage
SUMMER
BEFORE SENIOR YEAR

"IT'S SO FUCKING HOT OUT," I SAY, DROPPING INTO A SEAT OUTSIDE THE COFFEE SHOP where Declan and Braxton are already sitting and drinking their iced coffees. They've got a shit ton of papers strewn everywhere—lyrics, songs, and sheets of music—since we spend most of our time writing or playing music. When we graduate from high school in June, our goal is to get signed by Camden's parents' record label, Blackwood Records.

When I was little and banging on the drums my uncle bought me for Christmas, I never imagined I'd have a chance to play professionally one day. Every night, when my mom would leave for work, I'd use our neighbor's Wi-Fi to watch YouTube videos on how to play. I never thought it'd go anywhere until I met Camden, Declan, and Braxton, who were hell-bent on starting a band and in need of a drummer. I played for them—and Camden's dad—and learned, according to him, I was damn good, and if I stuck with them, I'd make a living one day from beating on those drums.

My thoughts go back to my uncle. He was the only decent person in my life... until he died from heart disease only a few short months before my mom died, leaving me alone in this fucking world.

"It's too damn hot," Declan agrees, snapping me from my thoughts as he lifts a paper and takes a look at a song Braxton wrote. "I think I saw it's going to be in the hundreds today." He drops the paper and takes a sip of his coffee. "Fuck, it's too hot to work on music."

"It's too hot to move," I say, wiping the sweat beading across my forehead. "Who the hell can even think in this heat?"

I've lived in New York my entire life, and I'm still not used to the few months a year when the heat waves come through and knock us all on our asses. Thankfully, fall and then winter will hit in a few months, and this ridiculous weather will be replaced with snow and ice. I'd take that over the humidity any day.

"You know what we should do?" Declan says, turning his phone around and showing us an image of a bunch of our classmates at the beach. I'm about to tell him he's lost his mind when I spot one classmate in particular. Bright red hair, piercing green eyes, and the body of a damn goddess, Tori Spears is the definition of a teenage wet dream.

"I'm in," I say without hesitation. I've had my eye on her for months. The only problem is, she and her best friends, Layla and Kaylee, have been on a no dating kick the past year since Layla's boyfriend cheated on her and broke her heart. Since the school year is over and we're about to start our senior year, I'm hoping that shit will be over, and I can slide in and take my chance.

"You don't even like any of those assholes," Braxton says with a laugh, reading my mind.

"I don't need to like them to get in the water and cool down." I stand, down the last of my iced coffee, and chuck the cup into the trash. "It's too hot to even smoke. Fuck it, let's go."

Declan chuckles. "He saw Tori in the picture. He's been eyeing that cheerleader for months."

"Tori?" Braxton says with a laugh. "Actually, I can totally see it. She's all cheerleader meets emo with her short skirts, black lipstick, and fishnet stockings. She's like the least peppy cheerleader on the squad. It's the perfect match made in hell."

Declan nods, and I punch Braxton in the arm. "Fuck you, asshole. Let's go."

A couple of hours later, we arrive at the beach. The place is packed, and I almost consider turning around and going home, but then I remember home fucking sucks, and Tori's here somewhere. After a few beats of scanning the area, I spot her, along with Kaylee and Layla, lying out in sexy as fuck bikinis surrounded by a bunch of jocks.

Layla glances up, noticing us first, followed by Kaylee and then Tori, whose gaze goes straight to me for several seconds before she turns back to her friends.

They whisper back and forth, and then a few seconds later, the three of them head our way. They're all in tiny as hell bathing suits, but once my eyes land on Tori, she's the only one I see. Sporting an all-black string bikini, she saunters straight over to me and wraps her arms around my neck, whispering, "Go with it," before her lips lock with mine.

The kiss is intense as fuck. Our mouths and tongues devour each other. She tastes sweet like mint, and as our kiss deepens, the gum responsible for her flavor ends up in my mouth. When she realizes what she did, she pulls back and laughs. "I'm so sorry. That was not supposed to happen."

"The kiss or sharing your gum?" *Because let's be real... I'm okay with both.*

"The gum," she says, her cheeks turning an adorable shade of pink. "The kiss was planned... well, as planned as it could be during our three-second conversation."

I glance over at my friends and notice Kaylee and Braxton are making out, and Layla and Declan are standing nearby laughing at whatever they're talking about.

"And to what do we owe the pleasure of getting kissed by the most beautiful cheerleaders on the squad?"

Tori snorts out a laugh. "The football players were totally trying to get in our pants." She scrunches her nose up in disgust. "We told them we had plans, and then you guys walked up, so when they asked with who, we said you guys. Perfect timing." She glances back and sees the guys have moved on to another group of women. "Seems like they bought it." She reaches up and kisses my cheek. "Thanks."

Just as she's about to turn and walk back to where Declan and Layla are now sitting, I grab her hip and pull her back toward me.

"You know what would be the perfect way to show your thanks?"

She quirks a single brow in response.

"Go out with me."

THANKSGIVING
SENIOR YEAR

"HOLY SHIT! YES, JUST LIKE THAT." TORI THROWS HER HEAD BACK AS I FUCK HER FROM THE bottom, hard and deep. The day after I asked her out, I took her to dinner and a movie with the only fifty bucks I had to my name.

By the end of the movie, we were dry fucking in the corner of the theater. The next night, she snuck me into her pool house, where we actually fucked, and shortly after, I was calling her my girl.

She's my first girlfriend, and I was worried I would suck at it, but she makes it easy. I don't know if it's because she knows I'm broke, but she never asks for shit. Always wants to hang out at her pool house, and simply being with me seems to be enough.

"Oh, God," she breathes as she comes down from her orgasm and slides off me so she can get cleaned up. "How soon until we can do that again?"

"Aren't we supposed to join your parents for dinner?" Unlike me, who comes from a home without a dad and a mom who sold herself on the street corner to make ends meet until she was found dead in a motel room when I was twelve, where I was then placed in the state's care and thrust into several foster homes, Tori's family is somewhat normal.

Her parents were in love until her dad passed away from a heart attack. Her mom remarried Tori's stepdad earlier this year, and they all live in a nice house in the Upper East Side. Tori only goes to the same school as us because she already attended our high school when her mom married her stepdad. She begged to stay with her friends, and her mom gave in.

"I told them I'm not feeling well," Tori says with a clipped tone I don't understand. Every time I'm around her parents, they seem nice, but Tori, for whatever reason, hates being around them. When I ask her about it, she says they're annoying, but it feels like there's more to it than that. I would give anything to have two parents who actually want to be around me... Hell, I would give anything to have a living parent, period.

"Tor..." I meet her in the bathroom and wrap my arms around her from behind. "It's Thanksgiving. Isn't it a day to be with your family?" Until I was invited to Camden's house for Thanksgiving last year, I never experienced an actual Thanksgiving dinner filled with family and friends and delicious food, but now that I have, I can't imagine not wanting it. Yet Tori would rather stay here, just the two of us, and miss out on the family and food.

I'm watching her in the mirror, so I catch her flinch, but before I can ask what's going on, she turns around and hops onto the counter, wrapping her arms and legs around me. "I'd rather spend today with you," she murmurs against my lips, "inside me."

And because I'd do anything she wants, instead of questioning her, I give in and spend the rest of the day inside her, just as she wants.

JANUARY
SENIOR YEAR

"I DON'T FEEL GOOD. PLEASE JUST LEAVE ME ALONE."

I've just returned from spending a week at Big Bear Mountain with Camden's family. I wanted her to go with us, but her parents said no. I offered to stay, but she insisted I go, not wanting to ruin my trip. I've never been there before or stayed in some crazy-expensive mansion/cabin. The trip was unreal. The guys and I spent the week skiing and snowboarding. It was the first real trip I've ever been on, and I hope when the band takes off, I can come back with Tori one day.

The moment we got home, I came straight here to see Tori, only to find her tucked into bed in the pool house. Her eyes are puffy, and her cheeks are stained pink like she's been crying, but aside from saying she doesn't feel good, she won't tell me what's wrong.

"Do you need medicine?" I ask.

"No," she chokes out. "I need you to leave me alone and let me sleep, please."

"Or I can lay with you while you sleep," I say, refusing to give up. I climb into her bed and wrap my arms around her from behind. At first, she stiffens at my touch, but after a few moments, she sighs and lets me hold her until she falls asleep.

FEBRUARY
SENIOR YEAR

"I'D LET YOU LIVE HERE," TORI SAYS, "BUT GLEN WOULD NEVER ALLOW IT." HER WORDS are slurred from the liquor she's been consuming and the weed we've been smoking.

I turned eighteen a few days ago, and the people who foster me made it clear I need to move out sooner rather than later since the money is about to stop, and as long as I'm there, they can't take in a younger kid, who will bring in more money. The state spouted some bullshit about helping me transition, but the last thing I want is any help from the same people who stuck me with that shitty-ass couple.

"It's all good," I tell her, kissing the corner of her mouth. "I'll figure something out."

"We could get our own place," she says, perking up. "We could get jobs and find a small apartment…"

"While going to school and playing in the band?" I shake my head. "We'd never make enough money. Besides, you're still seventeen, so there's no way your parents will let you move out. They'd kill us both."

Despite Tori trying to keep me away from her parents, I've been forced into several situations where we're all together during the past few months. While they seem nice, I've learned they can't stand me—especially her stepdad—and are hella strict. And not just like with a curfew, but about everything. Tori wants to go to school for dance, but her parents told her she'll be going for business, or they'll cut her off completely. They have no idea she's a cheerleader or that I'm in a band. They'd probably lock her ass up and stop her from seeing me altogether if they knew.

"Yeah," Tori mutters. "So what are you going to do?" She looks at me with glassy, sad eyes, and I pull her into my arms to kiss her soft lips. When we first started dating, Tori didn't smoke or drink, but now, it seems like she's high and drunk more than she's not. But since I am too, I guess I don't really have any room to judge.

"I just need to get through the next few months, and then, if all goes well, we'll be heading to LA." Tori's made it clear that she has no desire to major in business, and since she turns eighteen at the end of July, I told her she should just follow us over to the West Coast once she's legal and her parents can't give her any shit.

"I wish we could go now," she says softly. "I hate it here."

"In your pool house that your maid cleans and stocks with fresh food?" I joke. "There could be worse living conditions..."

"Fuck you, Gage," she snaps, sitting up and pushing me away. "You don't know anything about my life, so before you talk shit, maybe you should know the facts."

"Then tell me," I say, not shocked by her attitude. Tori's been lashing out at everyone in her life lately—especially me, since I'm the one around her the most—but she won't tell me what's going on. She just smokes and drinks, and once in a great while, she'll fuck me.

"I need to go," she says instead of answering. "My mom's having a stupid dinner for her birthday, and if I'm not there..." She doesn't finish her sentence. Instead, she stands and stumbles toward the bathroom. "You can see yourself out."

I sigh, wishing she would speak to me but knowing she won't. After getting dressed, I head over to Camden's, where his mom tells me I can stay with them as long as I promise not to smoke or drink in the house. I respect Sophia and Easton too much to ever do that shit around them, so I have no problem agreeing.

MAY

SENIOR YEAR

"I'M WORRIED ABOUT TORI." I'M SITTING IN HER PARENTS' LIVING ROOM. IT'S THE MIDDLE of the school day, but I took off so I could meet with them without Tori knowing. She's spiraling out of control, and I'm worried about her. She's stopped going to cheer, doesn't hang with her friends as much, and barely speaks to me. I don't know what's going on or how to help her. I know her parents can't stand me, but they love her, and I'm hoping they'll listen.

"We are too," Glen says. "She's been seeing a psychiatrist, who believes Tori has bipolar disorder. We've tried to put her on medications, but with her using drugs and drinking, they're causing her to lash out. Which is why we need your help."

I'm taken aback by everything they're saying since Tori has never said a word about any of this, but mostly, I'm shocked they actually want my help... until Tori's mom, Sandra, explains.

"We need you to break up with her, please," Sandra says. "We know you're planning to leave for LA once you graduate. We overheard you and Tori speaking, and if Tori goes, she'll never get the help she needs."

"Not happening," I say, realizing I made a mistake coming here.

"Please," Sandra pleads. "Tori is so lost, and as long as you're together, she won't let us help her."

"I love her," I choke out. "I can't just abandon her. She's my entire world. I get you don't like me, but I love her, and she loves me." I look at both of them, silently begging for them to understand. "I know we're young, but what we feel is real. I want her to get help, but please don't ask me to walk away from her. I can't do it. Not until she tells me that's what she wants."

Glen clenches his jaw. "Despite Tori trying to keep it from us, we know about your little band and how you're linked to the Blackwoods. If you want to pursue those dreams, I suggest you rethink your decision. End things with Tori and move on with your life. Otherwise, I'm going to be forced to make my own decisions that you're not going to like."

I stand, refusing to let this asshole threaten me. "Do what you got to do, but I'm not walking away from Tori."

"Please," Sandra begs as I walk toward the door. "If you love my daughter. If you want what's best for her, let her go."

MAY
PRE-GRADUATION PARTY

Tori: I won't be able to make it to the party. I'm sorry, Gage, for everything. But please know that I love you.

I STARE AT THE TEXT, CONFUSED AS FUCK. THIS IS THE LAST PARTY BEFORE WE GRADUATE, and the guys and I take off to LA. I asked Tori several times if she wanted to go, and she said she did. The more she pushes me away, the closer I pull her toward me. When I asked her about seeing a psychiatrist and being on meds, she lost her shit, telling me her parents were lying, and she wants to run away.

And when I told her I couldn't do that because she's still a minor, and I could get in serious shit, she accused me of being on their side. Despite me telling her she shouldn't smoke or drink, she got trashed, which led to us arguing until I ended up fucking the anger out of her. Since then, she's been quiet. Surprisingly, she hasn't been smoking or drinking lately, but she also hasn't been acting like herself. I just keep telling myself that once we're situated in LA, I'm going to bring her over there, away from her parents, and make sure she's taken care of. I love her and will do anything to make sure she's okay.

As I stare at her text, I consider texting her back but decide to just go over there. If I tell her I'm coming over, she'll argue and possibly leave. So instead, I pocket my phone and wallet, then head out.

Half an hour later, I arrive at Tori's house and head straight back to her pool house since that's where she spends all her time. I can't even remember the last time she actually spent the night in the main house.

Without knocking, since I never do, I enter the pool house. The first thing I notice is that it's quiet, which is unusual for Tori because, like me, she's one to blast music when she's alone.

"Tor!" I call out as I walk through the main room and down the hallway to the bedroom where she sleeps. "If you think I'm letting you stay home on the last night we have together, you have another—"

My words come to a halt, stuck in my throat, as I stare at the scene in front of me.

Tori.

Her lifeless body.

In the walk-in closet.

It takes several seconds for my brain to understand what I'm looking at, but once I do, I spring into action.

"Tori!" I shout as I quickly get her down and gently set her onto the floor. "Baby, what did you do?" Her body is cold… too cold, and her eyes aren't opening. "Tori, wake the fuck up!" I pat her cheeks, then drop my head to her chest to listen for a heartbeat. But there isn't one.

Refusing to give up, I call 911. While I wait, I try everything I can think of to bring her back to me. But she never wakes up.

When the paramedics arrive, they force me to step back, and when I do, my foot lands on something. I reach down and find it's a folded-up piece of paper with my name scrawled across the front. Needing to focus on Tori, I shove it into my pocket, praying to whatever fucking God there is that this is a mistake, a nightmare, that Tori will wake up, and I'll see those beautiful green eyes again.

Only she never wakes up.

And I never see her green eyes again.

When she's confirmed dead, it feels as though I've died right along with her.

One

Gage

SIX YEARS LATER

"FUCK, TORI, I CAN'T BELIEVE IT'S BEEN SIX DAMN YEARS SINCE THE LAST TIME I SAW your face, heard your voice, felt you in my arms." I glide my hand across the marble and release a harsh sigh. "You would've been twenty-four years old last week." I place a dozen flowers into the holder. "Sorry, I couldn't be here on your birthday. We were still on tour, and I couldn't figure out a way to get here and back without missing a show."

I drop onto my ass and close my eyes, wishing for the pain in my heart to go away. After all these years, you'd think the heart would be able to heal. But I swear, as I sit here and think about the only girl I've ever loved, my heart bleeds as badly as it did the day I lost her.

I've been busy for the past six years. After losing Tori, Easton put us on a plane to LA, where the guys and I signed a contract with Blackwood Records. A few months later, we released our first album and it blew the fuck up. We've been on several world tours, sold millions of songs and albums, and broken numerous records, but nothing relieves the constant pain deep in my soul over losing yet another woman I would've given my life to save.

"Sometimes, I wonder—" I start to speak, but my words are cut off by the sound of someone crying. Since I'm sitting in a cemetery, it's not uncommon to hear someone crying, but this cry… it's gut-wrenching like someone is literally pulling the soul out of one's body.

When I look around, I see a woman a few gravesites down lying across the ground with her arms draped over a headstone. Her body is visibly shaking, and her cries are heartbreaking.

I'm usually one to mind my own business, but something draws me to her. Maybe it's recognizing a kindred spirit, feeling the pain she feels.

When I walk over to her, I find her eyes are closed, and she's actually sleeping. She's crying, sobbing in her fucking sleep. I consider leaving her alone, but the sky is gray, and based on the dark clouds, it's due to rain soon.

Leaning down, I gently press my palm to her shoulder to nudge her awake. It only takes a few times before she jolts awake and faces me. Her dark red hair is up in a messy bun, and when her big green eyes meet mine, bloodshot and glassy and sad, so fucking sad, I'm momentarily taken aback. Aside from the similar hair and eye color, she looks nothing like Tori, but something in her eyes reminds me of Tori. Maybe it's the deep-seated devastation, silently begging someone to take her out of this world. I didn't see it in Tori when she was alive because I was young and wasn't looking for it. But after she was gone, I spent hours upon hours replaying every conversation we had, analyzing every word she spoke and didn't speak, wondering if I could've prevented her from ending her own life. I was too close to the situation to see it at the time, but when I look back, there were so many signs that I didn't see or pay attention to.

"Are you okay?" I ask the woman, who's barely looking at me.

She nods and is about to lie back down when I point out the obvious. "It's going to rain."

She doesn't even bother to look up at the sky, just nods again, then lies back down, wrapping her arms around the headstone like it's a blanket. She doesn't make any sound indicating that she's crying again, but her body wracks with silent sobs. And since she isn't my problem or my business, I walk away from her, knowing there's no way I can save her.

I snag a cab back to the apartment I share with my friends and bandmates, Declan and Braxton, and go straight to my bedroom, so I can light up a joint and lose myself in the high. When the high isn't enough, I pull some powder out and do a couple lines. The pain doesn't dull, but my head goes fuzzy enough to block it out a bit. With my headphones on and music blaring, I tune the world out, refusing to think about the sad as fuck woman crying at the cemetery. I couldn't save my mom, couldn't fucking save Tori, hell, I can't even save myself… I have no business thinking about that stranger or the pull that has me wanting to save her.

ONE WEEK LATER

AS I WALK THROUGH THE GATES OF ETERNAL CROSS CEMETERY, I TELL MYSELF I'M HERE because I miss Tori. And that is partially the truth. When I miss her, which is a helluva lot, I visit her, especially when we're in town. But if I'm honest, my reason for coming here today isn't completely about Tori. For the past week, that green-eyed woman has been on my mind. The way she looked at me—like, even though she was visiting someone else's grave, her life was the one that was over—called to me. I don't know anything about her, but I could feel her pain. I told myself to let it go, but here I am, heading back to visit Tori, wondering if I'll see that woman again.

I'm several yards away when I spot the woman who's been on my mind... along with two police officers. She's facing me, so I'm able to see the tears skating down her cheeks, but I can't hear what she's saying until I get closer.

"Please," she begs. "I can't leave. Please don't make me leave." She drops to the headstone and holds on to it like it's literally her lifeline as one of the officers bends to grab her arm.

"Ma'am, I'm sorry, but you need to leave."

"Hey!" I bark, making them all turn their attention to me. "Don't fucking touch her."

The officer stops reaching for her and stands. "Excuse me, sir. Do you know this woman?"

"Doesn't matter. You have no right to touch her or make her leave."

"Actually, we do," the other officer says. "She's been here for three weeks, and the manager called, requesting she leaves."

What the fuck? She's been here for three weeks? When I glance at her, I notice her hair isn't just messy, it's greasy, and her clothes are wet and dirty as if she's been stuck outside for... as the officer said, weeks. But still...

"This is a public place. You can't stop her from visiting."

"During visiting hours," the officer says. "But she's been refusing to leave, even when the cemetery is closed. A few people have complained, and the manager has asked that we escort her out. She can come back tomorrow, during visiting hours."

"So you're making her leave now... during visiting hours?"

"Visiting hours end in twenty minutes. She was warned yesterday that she needs to leave, but she refused."

"I can't leave him," she cries out. "Please don't make me leave him." She clutches the stone as liquid trails down her already tearstained cheeks.

"Ma'am, if you have nowhere to go, we can steer you in the direction of a shelter, but—"

"No, please," she continues to beg, and for the first time in years, the strings of my heart are tugged, making me realize my black, broken organ still works. "I miss him so much," she sobs. "I can't go home without him. I promise to be quiet. Please."

"You're not allowed to sleep here," the officer tells her. "I really am sorry, but if you don't leave on your own, we're going to have to detain you."

The woman's cries worsen, and without thinking, I step toward her, putting myself between her and the officers. "You're not taking her anywhere." Without giving her a chance to argue, I lift her into my arms and walk past the gentlemen as they watch me take her away.

I expect the woman to put up a fight about me carrying her, especially since I'm a damn stranger. Instead, she clings to me, sobbing that she doesn't want to leave him—I'm assuming him refers to the person's grave she's apparently been sleeping at for the past few weeks, refusing to leave.

"I know," I tell her, walking us to the front of the cemetery, "but those officers were going to arrest you, and then you wouldn't be able to stay with him anyway. Once they're gone, you can go back, okay?" She nods into my shoulder, her body trembling in devastation.

I flag down a cab, and once we're in the confined space, heading to my place, I get a whiff of her body odor. It's rough and proves what they said is true. She's been there for weeks without showering or changing her clothes. She's obviously left long enough to use the restroom and eat—though, she's tiny, which has me wondering how much she's actually eating.

She falls asleep in my arms and stays asleep as I carry her up to my apartment. I hate to wake her up, but she needs a good shower and a meal, so once we're in my bathroom, I gently nudge her until she opens her eyes. They're tired and sad and damn near lifeless, but unlike Tori and my mom, she's still alive... *For how long, though?*

"You need a shower," I tell her. "If you don't want me to see you naked, you're going to have to stand so you can do it yourself."

She stares at me... No, stares *through* me, and I know, despite her body being here, she isn't really here. I set her on the counter and, without looking, undress her and then turn the water on. In her back pocket, I feel something hard, so I pull it out and find her license and a credit card. Sadie Ruiz, born June 26th. Based on the year she was born, she's twenty-eight years old.

I set the cards down on the counter, and with my clothes still on, I step into the shower with her and wash her from head to toe. I scrub her hair a couple of times since it's been a while and soap as much of her body as I can without touching the parts I shouldn't touch.

"Can you wash yourself?" I ask her.

With her eyes barely open, she takes the washcloth from me, spreads her thighs slightly and wipes between her legs, then hands it back to me, closing her eyes. Figuring that's as good as it's going to get, I turn the water off and get out so I can get out of my wet clothes and into dry ones. Then I grab a towel and wrap her up in it, carrying her to my bedroom, where I put one of my shirts on her, along with a pair of my boxers.

Since she's barely awake, I lay her on my bed and cover her with the sheets so she can get a good night's sleep. Once she wakes up, I'll feed her, and then she can be on her way.

"NO! NO! PLEASE, FIX MY BABY! HE CAN'T BE GONE!"

The screams of terror have me jumping up from my seat—where I was sitting on the balcony and smoking a joint—and sprinting into the bedroom.

Sadie's eyes are closed, but her body flails from side to side. Fuck, she's stuck in a nightmare. Knowing about them all too well, I pull her into my arms, holding her tightly so she won't hurt me, and whisper for her to wake up.

She jolts awake, her eyes meeting mine. She's only been asleep for a few hours, but she already looks better. The sadness is still there, but she looks a little less tired.

"Who are you?" she breathes, her brows pinching together. "Where am I?" She tries to scramble out of my hold, so I let her go.

"I'm Gage, and you're in my apartment. The cops were going to arrest you for sleeping at the cemetery, so I brought you back here to shower and get some sleep."

Her features fall at the mention of the cemetery, and her eyes glass over as she edges off the bed and stands. "Thank you," she mutters, glancing down at my clothes. "I need to go back."

"Not tonight. They'll arrest you. You need to wait until at least tomorrow. It's two in the morning."

She sighs, tears filling her lids. "Maybe they won't notice."

"Or they'll be waiting to bust you, and you'll spend the night in jail and be charged with trespassing."

Understanding flits across her features. "Yeah, okay." She nods. "I'll just, um, get going…" As she speaks, her stomach rumbles so loudly it fills the room.

"You're not going anywhere." Her eyes go wide, and I realize I said that a bit too harshly. "It's late, and I'm not letting you leave in the middle of the night. Let me feed you, get a bit more sleep, and once it's morning, you can go." She contemplates this for a few beats before she nods in agreement.

The kitchen has food, but not much, so I make us both a bacon, egg, and cheese sandwich, which she devours in only a few bites. When I offer to make her another, she shakes her head.

"That's okay. I'd like to get some sleep if that's okay with you. Do you… have a guest room?"

"Nah, it's a three-bedroom place, and I have two roommates, but I can sleep on the couch—"

"No," she says, cutting me off. "I can. I don't mind."

"Not happening." I walk us back to my bedroom and turn the blankets down. "Get in and get some sleep."

She listens, climbing into the bed, but once she's in, she doesn't lie down. "Do you think you could lay with me? I know we don't know each other, but…" Tears fill her eyes. "I just have a hard time sleeping."

"No worries," I tell her, getting in and sliding next to her. She doesn't come closer, but she faces me, looking past me for several minutes until her eyes drift shut.

Once I know she's asleep, I get out of bed and go out onto the balcony to smoke. I'm only out here for maybe a half an hour when a soft, feminine voice has me turning around.

"Hey," she says, standing in the doorway, eyes filled with tears. "Bad dream?"

She nods, and I jut my chin, silently telling her to join me. She plops into the chair next to me, and I pass her my joint. For a second, she eyes it wearily, then takes a hit, choking on it slightly.

"First time?"

She glances over at me and shakes her head. "My husband used to smoke back in college, but it was never really my thing." She takes another hit, and her body relaxes. She hands it to me, and I take a hit before passing it back.

We take turns, silently passing the joint back and forth until her eyes are damn near closed, and I know the joint did what I was hoping it would do. It relaxed her enough to go to sleep.

I take one last hit, then pick her up and carry her to bed. As I watch her chest slowly rise and fall, I wonder where her husband is or if maybe he's the one she's mourning for. Then I push the thoughts away because Sadie isn't my business, and tomorrow, she'll be gone.

Two

Sadie

WHEN I WAKE UP WRAPPED IN SOFT SHEETS WITH A MAN SNORING SOFTLY NEXT TO ME, I forget where I am for a second. My brain automatically takes me back to before my entire world was taken from me, and for a split second, I imagine I'm in my bed, in my home. The man snoring is my husband, and it's only quiet because our son is still sleeping. My hand goes to my belly, and for a moment, I pretend there's a bump there, and my precious little girl is still growing safely inside. I lie still, enjoying a moment of reprieve, the escape, until there's a knock on the door, followed by, "Hey, Gage, I picked up breakfast. Get out here and eat... I miss you." My little escape is blown to pieces, and I'm back in reality.

No soft sheets.

No home.

No husband.

No son.

No baby growing in my belly.

I jolt up and glance at the guy apparently named Gage, but he doesn't stir at all.

"Gage, c'mon," the woman says. "I'm not letting you hide forever."

Making sure I'm dressed—which I am in clothes that definitely aren't mine—I drag myself out of the comfortable bed and quietly pad over to the door to make my escape. But before I open the door, I see my clothes folded in a neat pile in the corner with my license and bank card on top. I snag the pile and slip my sandals on, then open the door and step out, closing it quietly.

"Oh, hey," the pretty blonde says, still standing there. "I didn't know Gage had company. I'm Kaylee."

"Sadie," I murmur. "He's, um, still sleeping."

She gives me a once-over, and based on the look in her eyes, she's assuming I'm doing the walk of shame. I could correct her, but it doesn't really matter since I'll never see her again.

"There's plenty of food."

"Thank you, but I really need to get going."

"Okay."

Without another word, I leave as quickly as possible, not stopping until I'm outside the front of the building. I've lived in New York for the past ten years, since coming here for college, so I immediately recognize where I am and know which train I need to take to get back to where I belong.

Thirty minutes later, I walk through the gates of Eternal Cross Cemetery. I use their bathroom to change back into my freshly laundered clothes, and then I head straight over to where my entire world is.

"Hey, sweetheart, I'm sorry I left you." I choke up, something I do more often than not. "I can't promise I won't leave again since the mean people want to keep me from you, but I'll be here as long as I can be." I bring my two fingers to my lips, then place them on the headstone. "Mommy loves you so much."

Three

Gage

DON'T DO IT.

Mind your own fucking business.

That woman is not your damn problem.

You're not some superhero, for God's sake.

I tell myself all this and more, yet nothing I say stops me as I walk through the gates of the cemetery less than a week after I woke up to find Sadie and her clothes gone. I told myself it was for the best, and for a few days, I stayed away. But then I ran into Kaylee, and when she asked about Sadie, that prompted my thoughts to go to her. No matter how high or drunk I got, I couldn't push her out of my head.

I don't visit Tori often. It hurts too much. But that's the excuse I gave myself as I got dressed and headed out to the cemetery—I was going for Tori. But the truth is, I'm going to check on Sadie because I can't stop fucking thinking about her.

I just need to make sure she's okay, I tell myself. Once I know she isn't still sleeping in the cemetery at the grave of... whoever's grave it is she's sleeping at, I'll go.

Before I'm at Tori's grave, I know she's not here. The grave she was sleeping on is empty, and I sigh in relief. Good. She was just having a few rough weeks. I get it. If I wasn't in LA after Tori died, I probably would've done the same shit. Since I'm here, I walk over to Tori's grave to say hello. I end up spending a few hours here, but Sadie never shows, so I take off at dusk.

The next morning, I wake up and find myself at the cemetery again, telling myself that I just need to make sure she's okay. Once I know she is, I'll stop showing up. Like yesterday, Sadie isn't here, and by the time nightfall rolls around, it's clear she won't be showing up.

I'm about to take off when an older man and woman walk over to the grave Sadie was at. The woman drops to her knees and sobs as the guy lays flowers on not one but three graves lined up next to each other. They stay for a few minutes, talking quietly before they start to walk away.

I don't know why I do it, but before they get too far, I call out to them, making them turn around.

"I'm sorry to bother you. I just… I wanted to make sure Sadie's okay. I met her while she was here." I nod toward the graves they were just visiting.

The woman's brows shoot to her forehead, and the man frowns. "We're not sure how she is," the man says. "She won't speak to us."

"Sorry," I say dumbly, unsure how else to respond.

"Do you know Sadie well?" the woman asks.

"Nah, just seen her here a couple of times."

"She, umm…" The gentleman clears his throat. "She's been detained at the NYPD. We tried to get her out, but aside from her not wanting our help, they denied her bail."

Fuck. "For sleeping here?"

The woman nods as fresh tears fill her eyes. "It was all my fault," she cries out.

"Stop, honey," the man says, pulling her into a hug. When the woman's cries deepen, he apologizes and says he needs to get her home.

As soon as they're gone, I go to the front office and demand to speak to the manager. "Did you have Sadie Ruiz arrested?"

"I cannot speak about this matter," the manager says, sticking his nose into the air like he's better than me. Well, we'll see about that...

I stalk out of the office and pull my cell phone out, dialing Easton.

"Gage, everything okay?"

"No, a... friend of mine has been detained at the NYPD. I'm on my way there, so I don't know the specifics, but I know you're good friends with that judge... I wouldn't ask but..."

"I'll give him a call now," Easton says. "Text me his name."

"It's actually a *her*."

Easton's quiet for a moment, but thankfully doesn't question me on it. "Text me her info and I'll see what I can do."

Two hours later, Sadie is released with a warning, thanks to Easton's friend, Daniel Maxwell. She has to promise not to sleep at the cemetery anymore, and despite not wanting to agree to that, she does, understanding that the next time she's arrested, she can be forced to serve ninety or more days in jail.

"Thank you," she says as we walk out of the courthouse and over to the car I have waiting for us. It's not often I use our car service, but it was easier than dealing with cabs, and since I was going to be in a public place, I had to take security with me to be on the safe side.

"No problem. Where do you want to be dropped off?" I ask,

already knowing what she'll say.

"The cemetery please."

We arrive a little while later, and she gets out, thanking me again. But before I let her go, I ask a question that's been on my mind. "Are you homeless?"

She doesn't even look surprised by my question when she says, "I can't go home."

"So you do have a home then?"

She shakes her head, not giving me anything more.

"You can't sleep here anymore. Easton pulled a shit ton of strings to get you out, and if you get arrested again, he won't be able to save you."

"I know," she murmurs. "I'll figure something out. Thank you, again."

She closes the door, not waiting for my response, and I tell my driver to go. Sadie isn't my damn problem...

And that's what I'm still telling myself several hours later as I'm pulling back up to the cemetery to make sure she isn't doing anything stupid like trying to sleep here.

Of course, I find her doing just that. Lying across the middle of two of the three graves those people laid flowers on and crying softly. Since she only has a few minutes before the manager will no doubt be out here to make sure she's gone, I sit next to her and say, "You need to say goodbye."

"I can't," she says, "it's too hard."

"Just for the night, Sadie," I remind her. "You can come back tomorrow."

She nods, then sits up, wiping her tears.

Since this is the first time I've ever sat over here, I take a moment to read the headstones, noticing that all three have the same last name—the same last name as her.

Jesus, fuck. All of these are her family?

As if she can sense my question, without tearing her eyes away from the graves, she says, "In one day, I lost my entire world."

Four

Sadie
FIVE WEEKS EARLIER

"MOMMY, CAN WE GET LOTS OF FIREWORKS FOR THE FOURTH OF JULY?" COLLIN, MY FOUR-year-old son, asks, jumping up and down as I push the shopping cart down the grocery store aisle. His dark red hair, identical to mine, flops across his forehead, in need of a cut. I make a mental note to call to schedule an appointment.

"Of course," I tell him, pushing the strands out of his eyes. "But I'm going to let your daddy handle that."

Collin frowns. "Daddy's at work. Can't we get them now? What if they sell them all, and then there's nothing left?"

"He'll be off all weekend, and I promise they won't sell out." I reach on the top shelf for the pasta Collin loves as a sharp pain radiates through me, making me clutch my belly and take a deep breath. I'm twenty-six weeks pregnant, but I've been having annoying pains during the entire pregnancy. The doctor says they're growing pains, and when I mentioned I didn't get them with Collin, she pointed out that every pregnancy is different.

"Mommy, are you okay?" Collin asks, his features etched with concern.

"Yes, sweetie. I'm okay," I tell him, leaning over and kissing the top of his head. "What do you say we check out, and when we get home, I'll make some sandwiches to bring to Daddy's work? I bet we can convince him to leave early and go buy all the fireworks."

I wink playfully, and Collin's face lights up in excitement. "Yes!"

Once the groceries are brought in and put away, I go about making the sandwiches, with Collin's help, then text Vincent to make sure he's at work.

Vincent: I'm here and hungry. Can't wait to see you guys. Thanks, baby. Love you.

Since we found out I'm pregnant, he's been trying so hard to stay on the right track. Unfortunately, because of his track record, I'm reluctant to give him the benefit of the doubt, but I will say it's been close to four months since, according to him, he's touched a single pill. And he goes to his NA meetings several times a week. It's going to take longer than that to prove he's serious about staying clean, but I hope, for our family's sake, he does.

Me: Love you too. See you soon.

Because we live just outside of the city in the suburbs, it's too far to walk to the train station, and the investment firm Vincent's family owns is in the city, so we drive when we have to go into the city. It's annoying, with all the ridiculous traffic, but I try not to go as often as possible, preferring to spend my time in the quietness of the 'burbs.

An aching pressure pushes down on my bladder, and I hand the basket to Collin, telling him to put it in the car while I go pee. Only when I wipe myself and find a good amount of blood on the toilet paper, I know we won't be going to see Vincent today. I close my eyes and say a silent prayer that the baby is okay, but deep down, I know it's not.

Grabbing a pad, I line my underwear and then call my doctor, who tells me to go straight to the hospital. Next, I call Janice, my mother-in-law. "Something's wrong," I tell her. "I'm going to go to the hospital, but I don't want to take Collin."

"I'll be right there."

After hanging up, I call Vincent, who tells me he'll meet me there. It's not ideal for me to drive, but it would take too long for him to drive home, only to drive back out to the city where my doctor is located.

Less than an hour later, we find out our baby, our precious little girl has no heartbeat, and because I'm so far along, I have to give birth. It's the worst night of my life, and by the time we're leaving the hospital, we're both so filled with grief that neither of us says a word to each other. Usually, when you go to the hospital and give birth, you come home with a baby, but when we arrive, we're empty-handed. And because of how far along I was, decisions need to be made. Do we cremate or bury her?

Collin is asleep in his bed when we arrive at the house, so I tiptoe in and place a soft kiss on his temple. "I love you, baby boy," I murmur, the pain in my heart healing a tiny bit at the sight of my sweet boy.

He stirs and mutters, "I love you too," but he's too deep in his sleep to actually wake up. He was looking forward to having a little sister, and I dread having to tell him that we lost her before we even got her.

After thanking Janice for watching Collin, and her insisting on spending the night, I excuse myself, so I can privately mourn for the baby I've lost. As I pass Vincent's home office, I stop in the doorway.

"It's late. Come to bed, please." I could really use him right now.

Holding me and telling me everything will be okay.

He glances up at me, his eyes bloodshot. "In a little bit. I need... a moment."

"Vince..."

"Sadie, just give me a few minutes."

I nod, praying our loss doesn't send him spiraling back down, and retreat to our room. I don't know how long I'm asleep, but when I wake up, I'm a bit disoriented. The first thing I notice is that light is shining in through the slats of the blinds, so it must be morning. Then I notice my mother-in-law is sitting on the edge of the bed, crying.

I assume it's because of the baby we've lost until she says, "I'm so sorry. I never should've left."

"Left to go where?" I ask, sitting up and wiping the sleep from my eyes.

"Oh, God," she sobs. "I'm so, so sorry. I can't believe this happened. I'll never forgive myself."

"What's going on?" I ask, my heart picking up speed in my chest. Like a mother's intuition, I can feel deep in my gut that something is wrong, very wrong.

"I left to take Henry some papers," she cries out. "I told Vincent I would be back soon. I don't know why he left... but he did... They're gone, Sadie. They're both gone."

"Where did they go?" I ask, somehow already knowing the answer but refusing to understand. "Where did they go?" I scream, jumping out of bed and ignoring the pain from giving birth only hours ago.

"I don't know," she says, shaking her head. "We don't know anything except that they're both gone. The police and the hospital tried to call you, and when you didn't pick up, they called me. I'm so sorry, Sadie. They were in a car accident and brought to the hospital.

The doctors did all they could, but they didn't make it. I'm so sorry." She sobs. "They're both gone."

PRESENT DAY

"YOU LOST YOUR UNBORN BABY, YOUR SON, AND YOUR HUSBAND ON THE SAME DAY?" Gage says slowly.

"Well, technically not all in the same day, but within twelve hours of each other, yeah." My eyes go to the three graves: my husband, my son, and my baby girl. "He swore he wasn't taking any more pills, but he lied. The autopsy report showed traces of them in his system. He knew better than to drive our son anywhere, but he wasn't thinking. We were both grieving. I'm not making excuses for him, but I'd like to believe that he wouldn't have left with our son if he was thinking clearly. They found breakfast and two coffees in the car. He must've taken Collin to get us all breakfast and thought he would be okay," I choke out. "According to the street cam, he ran a red light and hit another vehicle. It was a large truck, and the guy survived, but Vincent and"—emotion fills my throat, making it hard to speak—"Collin died on impact."

Gage pulls me tighter into his arms, and I cry into his chest. I don't know anything about this man aside from the fact that he seems to care about me enough to keep saving me, but I don't have it in me to care that I'm leaning on a total stranger.

"Sometimes, I wish I wasn't alive," I admit out loud for the first time. "My heart aches so badly, and I wish I could just turn it all off."

Gage's hold on me tightens. "I know exactly how you feel."

After I cry for a little while longer, Gage carries me to the SUV he drove here and takes me back to his place. He forces me to eat and then shower, and when I get out, I find him sitting on the balcony smoking a joint.

"Mind if I join you?" I ask, stepping outside.

He answers by taking a hit and then stretching out his hand in proffer. Because I have nothing left to lose, I accept it and take a hit, allowing the weed to calm my body. After several hits, my body is numb, and I can't feel anything. I know this is a dangerous game I'm playing. I watched Vincent suffer with addiction, but I just don't have it in me to give a shit. I've lost everyone I love, leaving me with nothing and no one to live for. For just a little while, maybe it's okay to allow myself to be numb, to turn it all off temporarily. It sure as hell beats the constant pain I feel.

We sit outside, passing the joint back and forth, until my eyes start to droop. Then Gage insists we head to bed. I snuggle into the sheets and close my eyes as he joins me, spooning me from behind. I'm just about asleep when I hear the sound of his drawer opening and closing. A pill bottle being opened, and then the distinct sound of him swallowing.

Pills… He's an addict. *Just like my husband* is my final thought before I allow myself to fall into a fitful sleep where I dream about my life before I lost everything.

And for the next several weeks, our routine seems to run on a loop. During the day, I visit the graves, refusing to leave my son and daughter. When it gets late, Gage comes and gets me. We eat and smoke and eventually pass out. Until the last week in September, when I wake up and see what the date is. Then everything changes…

"CAN WE STOP BY THE STORE?" I ASK ON OUR WAY TO THE CEMETERY. GAGE GIVES ME A confused look, most likely because, aside from asking to pick up tampons last week, I never ask for anything since there's nothing I need.

"Today's… Collin's birthday," I tell him, hating that after all this time, I still can't say my son's name without my throat clogging with emotion and tears filling my eyes. "I'd like to get him a cake. His favorite is…" I clear my throat. "*Was* vanilla with buttercream icing."

Gage nods and takes a detour to the store. Using my card, I purchase a small cake and have *Happy Birthday, Collin* written on it.

"He would've been five years old today," I tell Gage as we sit on the balcony later that evening. We never talk about anything, but not talking about my son, the best part of me, on his birthday feels wrong. "He was so excited to start school, but because his birthday is after the cutoff date, he had to wait an extra year." A choked sob pushes up my throat. "He never got to go to school."

My eyes meet Gage's, and he nods in acknowledgment, not bothering to say anything since there's nothing for him to say.

"He loved Batman," I continue. Even though it hurts like hell to think about him, I'm afraid if I don't talk about him, no one will, and my little boy deserves to be thought about, spoken about, on his birthday. "And riding his bike. We would ride for hours along the streets of our neighborhood."

My sobs strengthen, but I can't stop. "He was so smart and caring and…" Fuck! "He should be here!" I slam my fist on the table. "He should be here! His father's job was to protect him, and instead, he killed him, and now, on his birthday, he's not here!"

Between my screaming and crying and despite being high as hell, I quickly spiral into a panic attack that has Gage picking me up and carrying me to the bed. But tonight, the weed isn't enough…

"I need you," I beg, wrapping my arms around his neck. "Just for tonight, I need you to make me forget."

"Sadie," he groans, shaking his head. "I can't be that person for you."

"I need you to help me escape," I beg. "Help me *feel* something other than pain. Please."

He stares at me for a long moment as if contemplating what to do, and just when I think he's going to reject me, his mouth crashes down on mine. He tastes a mixture of spicy like the alcohol he was drinking and smoky like the weed we were smoking, and I focus on that, allowing myself a moment of reprieve. The kiss isn't sweet or gentle. It's rough and hard, and everything, at this moment, I didn't even realize I needed. I've gone months without feeling wanted or needed or desired. My only emotion has been constant pain.

Needing to feel something else, something more, even if I allow myself to get lost in Gage for a short time. Our clothes are ripped off, and hands are everywhere, all over each other. Mine grab for his dick while his massage my breast. His mouth sucks on my neck, my throat, then wraps around my nipple, biting hard and making me squirm. Vincent was always gentle, loving... Most of the time, he was apologizing for messing up. But Gage is unapologetically rough, and it's exactly what I need.

He glides down my body, finding my center, and pushes a couple of digits deep into me. If I wasn't so wet, it'd probably hurt, but I'm soaked, and as he pumps in and out of me, that's proven by the sound of my slickness reverberating throughout the otherwise quiet room.

As my orgasm slams into me, I hold on to it for dear life, wanting to latch on to this moment of euphoria, where the short-lived bliss overpowers the agony and devastation I know are waiting for me.

I'm still flying high from my climax, panting unabashedly, when

Gage spreads my legs and thrusts into me. His fingers wrap around my throat, and his mouth slants across mine, his tongue delving past my parted lips. He fucks me with abandon, siphoning pleasure from my body... pleasure I freely give him. I want him to temporarily feel as good as I do, knowing that once this ends, we'll both be right back where we were, in pain that shows no hope of letting up.

Gage shocks me by reaching between us and finding my clit once again. We both come long and hard, and between the high of the orgasms and the weed, I'm barely able to keep my eyes open long enough to see him pull out and grab a washcloth to clean me.

Still naked, we both fall asleep, our bodies wrapped up in one another, and for the first time since I lost my entire world, I sleep all night without a single dream or nightmare. And just like that, I've found my new escape, my own addiction.

And for the next couple of weeks, it works... until everything changes once again.

Five

Gage

"CAN I ASK YOU A QUESTION?"

I glance over at Sadie, whose eyes were just closed but are now open. Over the past couple of months, I've learned that she has trouble sleeping. And since I know firsthand nothing can cure what we have—a broken heart—I do what I can to help. When she can't fall asleep, she likes to ask questions. So I answer them, and at some point, while I'm talking, she'll pass out. When she has nightmares, I'll pull her into my side to try to comfort her. She'll sigh against me as if my presence reminds her that wherever she was in her dream wasn't real, and within seconds, she'll pass back out. And when she wakes up early, she likes to take a warm bath. When she does this, I'll hear her crying from inside the bathroom, so I give her space.

Tonight, it looks like questions it is.

"You know you can," I tell her, pausing the TV and rolling onto my side to face her.

"Why don't you ever work?"

Until now, her questions have been about bullshit topics like my favorite color and food or my favorite subject in school. She's made it a point not to broach any topics that cause either of us to delve too deep. Until now…

But in her defense, this question isn't really deep. And since I live in a three-bedroom apartment in one of the nicer areas of New York and have yet to leave her side in the two months we've been chilling together, it's a valid question. But it's one I'm not prepared to answer. Telling her I'm in a band might change our dynamic, something I don't want to happen because… I like Sadie. More than that, I like her company. She doesn't judge or question shit. She just rolls with the flow.

For years, I've felt like an outsider with my friends, especially as of late—with Camden and Braxton finding their significant others and settling down. Declan's single, but he hangs out with Kendall—Camden's sister and Declan's love interest—a lot. And when we're all together, they look at me like I'm a broken toy they need to fix.

But Sadie doesn't see me like that. She knows I'm broken, but she accepts me the way I am. We could spend an entire day watching shows, laughing about nothing—something that's rare for her—to laugh that is—or we can go an entire day without saying a word, and both days she's content to just… be.

But I'm worried once she knows who I am, shit might change. She might not see me the same way as she does now, or she'll ask more questions that will lead to topics I don't want to touch.

When I don't answer quickly enough, she says, "Sorry, I didn't mean to overstep," and fuck if that doesn't make me like her that much more.

"You're not," I say, reaching out without thought and pushing a few strands of her dark red hair behind her ear that have fallen out of her messy bun. "I'm taking some time off." Not a lie since the band is taking a little break after our tour, and Camden and Layla just had a baby. "I have some money saved up, so I'm living off that until I figure out what's next." Also, not a lie.

Of course, she takes the answer at face value, nodding in understanding. "I've been thinking about the future," she says, shocking the hell out of me. While she loves to ask questions, she never usually talks about herself. "I got my degree in English and was working as an editor when I got pregnant with…" She swallows thickly. "When I got pregnant with Collin. Because Vincent made more than enough money, I decided to be a stay-at-home mom. But I'm thinking now, that… I have…" Tears fill her eyes, and she gets so choked up she's unable to finish her sentence. I pull her into my arms and hold her tight as she cries softly into my chest.

"You don't have to figure shit out right now," I say. "Just… let yourself grieve."

"OH, GOD, YES, JUST LIKE THAT."

I know I've hit the spot when Sadie's eyes roll up to the ceiling. Her back arches, and her tight cunt squeezes the fuck out of my dick, taking me straight over that edge right along with her.

I pull out and drop onto my back, needing to catch my breath. Fuck, I'm out of shape. I can't even remember the last time I worked out. Maybe it's because I've never been with the same woman more than once since… Well, I had no idea how insatiable women could be. At least Sadie is. Ever since the first time we fucked, she's wanted it on the regular. Since she's the one grieving, I don't want to take advantage and am never the one to start it, but to be honest, I don't even need to because she wants it all the damn time… Not that I'm complaining.

My phone dings with a text, and I glance at it, seeing Camden's name, along with a picture of his newborn daughter, Marianna. She was born a couple of days ago, and I was supposed to go up to the hospital to visit. I tried, but the moment the car pulled into the hospital parking lot, flashbacks of the worst fucking night of my life hit me so hard, I made the driver turn around and take us back to the condo, where Sadie and I spent the next two days getting high and fucking.

I text Camden back, telling him she's beautiful, but don't make any promise of coming to visit, knowing that shit isn't happening until they're back at home.

"I need to clean up," Sadie murmurs, sliding off the bed and stumbling to the bathroom, still high from the joint we shared earlier.

I open my bedstand drawer and grab the baggie of powder, dropping some onto the wood. Using the razor, I form a line and then lean in, taking a hit. The high is instant, but it's not enough, so I do one more line before I get up to get dressed.

"I'm gonna take a shower," Sadie calls from inside the bathroom, poking her head out. "Wanna join?"

"Nah, I'm gonna get a drink and make something to eat. You hungry?"

"Starved," she groans. "I'll just be a few minutes."

After taking a piss, I throw on my shorts and pad out to the kitchen to see what I can whip up. I'm scouring through the fridge when the front door alarm goes off, and seconds later, Braxton and Declan join me in the kitchen.

"'Sup," I say, grabbing some bread to make Sadie and me a couple of grilled cheeses.

"Just came from visiting the baby. They're back at home, so we stopped by to bring them some food. Have you gone by to see them?" Declan asks, his tone filled with accusation.

Without meeting his eyes, I shake my head, not wanting him to see the truth… That I couldn't fucking do it.

"Nah, I forgot," I lie. "But Camden sent me a picture. Cute kid. I'll go by and see them soon."

I can feel Declan glaring my way, but I ignore him, focusing on buttering the bread and heating up the pan.

"How's Kaylee?" I ask Braxton, referring to his girlfriend, who I'm friends with. Some bullshit went down the other night with his dad paying off Braxton's bodyguard to seduce her, which ended in her being drugged and a bunch of photos being posted that made it look like she was cheating on him—which was a fucking lie because she wouldn't do that shit to him.

"She's all right," Braxton says. "Still a little shaken up, but we'll get through it. She's actually why I stopped by. I wanted to talk to you both."

I set the sandwiches in the pan to cook and look up. "What's up?"

"I've convinced Kaylee to let me move in with her." Braxton grins, and my heart clenches in my chest, happy for him and Kaylee. They've been in love with each other for years, and I'm glad they're finally working shit out. They both deserve to be happy.

"Congrats, man!" Declan hugs him.

"Congrats," I add, flipping the sandwiches over.

"Thanks." Braxton smiles, looking happy as hell. "I had planned to give her space and let her live alone for a while, but—"

"But you can't stay away from her, so you're ditching this bachelor pad to move in with your girlfriend," Declan finishes.

"Yeah." Braxton shrugs. "Pretty much."

"It's all good," Declan says. "Speaking of which…" He turns his attention on me. "The lease is due to renew soon. You still want to live here, or are you planning to ditch me too?"

I scoop up the sandwiches and drop them onto the plates. "Where the fuck am I going?" I ask, confused as shit.

"I don't know," Declan says slowly. "You and Sadie have been chilling for a minute, so I wasn't sure if you guys were wanting your own space or if she's planning to officially move in."

When I glare at him, wondering where the fuck this is coming from, he raises his hands in mock surrender. "What? I'm just saying, if you want Sadie to move in, I'm okay with that. If you guys want your own place so you can fuck somewhere other than the bedroom, I'm not about to cock block." He shrugs.

"It's not like that," I mutter.

"Gage," Declan says softly. "You know it's okay to move on, right? It's nice seeing you with someone since Tori died. You deserve to be happy."

The mention of Tori causes a huge fucking ball of emotion to clog my throat, making it hard to breathe. One second, I was making a goddamn sandwich, and the next, I'm struggling to find my next breath. My heart picks up speed, pounding so hard behind my rib cage that it feels as though my entire body is pulsating.

"Gage, you okay?" Braxton asks, but I'm too lost in my thoughts to respond. My hands are clammy, and my body breaks into a cold sweat. Fuck! Did I have a bad hit? But even as I mentally ask the question, I know it's not the coke. It's me…

"Gage…" I vaguely hear Braxton and Declan talking, but the blood roaring in my ears drowns out the words.

Tori.

Moving on.

Sadie.

Happy.

No. No. No. Fucking no.

That's not what's going on with Sadie. She's grieving like me and needed a place to crash. We're smoking, chilling, fucking. It's nothing more than that. I'm not capable of anything more than that.

Sandwiches and friends forgotten, I stumble down the hallway, needing some space. Some fresh air. Needing to get high and make all these thoughts go away.

When I get in my room, I grab a joint from my drawer and am walking to my balcony when Sadie exits the bathroom, dressed in nothing but my shirt and some tiny as fuck panties.

"Hey," she says, smiling softly, her green eyes warmly meeting mine. She saunters over, wrapping her arms around my neck and kissing my lips. "Where's the food?"

My heart swells in my chest, and I push her away. "What are we doing?" I choke out.

Her lips turn down into a frown. "Umm… I thought we were going to eat. Are you not hungry?"

"No." I shake my head, stepping back. "What are *we* doing?"

She opens her mouth then closes it, unsure of what to say. "Umm, we just had sex," she says slowly. "I figured we would eat and then go to bed. It's late… Are you feeling okay?" She brings her palm up to my face, but I move before she can touch me.

Her worried tone. Her sad, confused eyes.

"Gage, talk to me," she says, and I can hear it in her voice. She cares about me.

I glance around, taking in my room. Her lotion is on my nightstand, her clothes are hanging over my chair. The TV is paused on her show. She's become a part of my life.

Our routine. The cemetery, the talking and fucking.

This wasn't supposed to happen.

I warned her. I told her I couldn't be that guy.

She said she understood.

"Gage, you're scaring me," she says, her voice cracking. "What's going on with you? Did something happen?"

This woman is grieving. She's lost her entire fucking world and has nothing left to live for. No reason to give a shit about anyone or anything. Yet here she is, worried about me. Caring about me.

My eyes lock with hers, and for a moment, my future flashes before my eyes.

Letting her in.

Letting her love me.

Loving the hell out of her.

Creating a life with her.

All I ever wanted was to create a life with you…

Tori's letter…

My hands hit my knees as her last words to me play back in my head.

Dear Gage,

Let me first start by saying how much I love you. If you're reading this, it's because I'm gone, and for that, I'm sorry. They say suicide is a selfish act, and I never understood that until now because even as I write this letter to you, the only guilt I feel about ending my life is that I'm hurting you. You're not only my boyfriend but also my best friend, which is why it's so hard to write this letter. There are some things you need to know. But, before I tell you, I need you to promise that you won't tell anyone. I'm only telling you so you understand that my taking my life isn't because of you. If anything, the only reason I didn't do it sooner was because of you. Because of how much I love you. Every time I imagined my future, it was with you. All I ever wanted was to create a life with you. I thought

I could be strong, but I'm not. I'm weak.
What I'm about to tell you needs to stay between you and me. Once you're done reading this letter, I want you to burn it. Then get on a plane and go to LA and become the best damn drummer the music industry has ever seen. Promise me, please. Do this for me. Nothing will bring me back, and I don't want you to ruin your life because of him.
Glen. For the past several months, he's been coming into the pool house when you're not here and raping me. I know what you're thinking. Why didn't I tell you? For a couple of reasons. One, I was scared of what you'd do. I know how much you love me and would do anything to protect me, and I couldn't put you in that position. I went to my mom. I thought she would believe me and protect me like a mom is supposed to, but instead, she said that I'm sick and need help.
And then I heard them talking. You went to them and begged them to help me. God, I love you for that, but there's no helping me because they don't want to help me. They want me gone. Glen is planning to run for mayor, and he sees me as a loose string. He's planning to send me away, and if you stand in his way, he's going to ruin you. He's rich and has connections, and I can't let him ruin you like he's ruined me...

"Fuck!" I bark out, fisting my hair. "No more!" I can't hear the words in my head anymore. Can't replay that fucking letter for the millionth time. I can't finish her thoughts. Her confessions. I can't finish the rest of the letter. For years, I've blocked the words out, and now they're rushing back, filling my head and heart, and I can't fucking do it.

I need to get high. I need to escape.

"Gage, what are you doing?" Sadie asks.

"I gotta go."

"What? Where?"

"Out!" I snap as I throw on a shirt, grab my wallet, and then stalk out of the room and the apartment. I faintly hear Sadie calling my name. She's confused since I've never gone anywhere without her, but I don't stop. Because if I do, I might lose the guts to do what I need to do.

I failed my mom, failed Tori, and I have no doubt if I let Sadie in, I'll fail her too. She's been hurt enough, has lost enough. The last thing she needs is to be dragged down into hell with me.

I repeat those words to myself over and over again on my way to the club. I keep repeating them once I'm there and the manager escorts me to the VIP loft. The words play on loop as I snort line after line of coke. And it's only once the needle enters my arm that the words as well as everything else finally go silent.

Six

Sadie

STARTLING AWAKE, I GLANCE AT THE WINDOW, THE DARKNESS REVEALING THAT IT'S either still nighttime or early morning. My hands glide across the sheets. Cold. Gage never came to bed. As I press the button on the remote to flash the time, a noise from the living room grabs my attention.

4:00 a.m.

After Gage freaked out and left, I tried to stay awake to wait for him. Because I don't have a phone, nor do I know his number, I couldn't call or text him. But at some point, I must've fallen asleep.

Another noise has me sliding off the bed and padding out to the living room to see if it's him. His roommates, Declan and Braxton, are rarely home, and when they are, they spend most of their time in their rooms. I've only run into them a couple of times, but they seem like nice guys. When they've seen me, they smile and say hello, and despite feeling dead inside, I make it a point to smile and say hello back.

The noise gets louder, and I wonder if maybe someone is

watching TV in the living room. I consider remaining in Gage's room, not wanting to intrude, but my throat is dry, and I could use a bottle of water. Really, I want to see if it's Gage. Maybe he came home and fell asleep on the couch. I don't know what got into him before he left, but it's so unlike Gage. During the short time I've known him, he's always been so calm and collected. Not once has he ever raised his voice or freaked out the way he did last night.

When the noise increases, I decide to take my chances and go out there. Worst-case scenario, I turn around and come back to the room. But if Gage is sleeping on the couch, I want him to know he can come to bed. This is his place, after all, and if I'm honest with myself, I like sleeping with him. He makes me feel a little less alone, especially when he pulls me into his side and holds me until I fall asleep in his arms.

The moment I step out of the room, I regret it. I wish I could go back inside and remain ignorant. Go back to sleep. Pretend I didn't hear anything. But that's the thing about life: there's no going back. If I could, I would've forced my husband to get more help. I wouldn't have accepted his word when he promised he would never pop another pill. And when we lost our daughter, instead of locking myself in my room to grieve, I would've pulled him and our son into my arms and held them tight, refusing to let them go. I would've made sure Vincent was okay instead of focusing on myself, on my mourning.

But that's not how it works. Every action has a consequence. And we can't predict how any situation is going to play out. But what we can do… is learn from our mistakes. Which is what I'm about to do right now.

As I stare at the scene in front of me, I take it all in. Gage is sprawled out on the couch, his pants unzipped and his head back, eyes closed, as a woman kneels between his legs, bobbing her head up and down while making the loudest slurping sounds I've ever heard. My stomach tightens and roils, and I worry I'm going to throw up right here, all over the floor.

The other woman—yes, there are two—sits next to Gage with her dress bunched at her waist. Her thighs are spread wide, showing everything between her legs as she fingers herself, making noises of pleasure. With the hand that she's not using, she drags her fingers through Gage's curly locks and fists his hair, pulling his face toward hers. His eyes remain closed as their mouths connect, and they both find their release.

My heart… my battered and bleeding heart feels as though it's stuck in my throat, blocking my airway as I continue to watch the scene unfold.

The woman who was just sucking Gage's dick stands and reaches into Gage's pocket, pulling out a small baggie. She spreads the powder on the table and then dips her head and does a line.

"Come on, baby," she coos, "your turn."

As Gage lifts his head, his hooded lids lazily flutter open, and our gazes clash. His eyes are lifeless and glassed over, and even though it seems like he's looking at me, it's almost as if he's looking through me.

"Gage," I breathe, tears filling my eyes as it hits me. As much as it breaks my heart to see him with other women, we're not together. We never made any promises to each other. Gage made it clear that he couldn't be that guy for me. He warned me, but I didn't want to listen, too caught up in my own grief.

But I have to listen now because as much as I care about Gage, as much as I appreciate him taking me in and helping me through the worst time in my life… I can't do this. I can barely save myself, let alone him, and I can't put myself in this position again. Unlike my husband who lied to my face, Gage has been honest. He doesn't hide the weed or the coke. He told me, flat-out told me, he couldn't be that guy.

Gage is a drug addict, and I learned the hard way that I can't compete with the drugs. I tried once, and I lost everything. So I can't do that again. This means I only have one option: I have to leave, so I can save myself.

Breaking our eye contact, I go back to the bedroom and get dressed. Since I don't have anything here but a few outfits and toiletries, I don't take anything with me. But before I go, I spot a journal on the nightstand. Gage writes in it sometimes...

Grabbing a pen, I rip a sheet out and pen a short note to him.

Gage,
Thank you for being there for me when I had no one else. You took a broken stranger in and saved me from myself. I wish there was some way I could return the favor, but I don't have anything to offer you. I hope one day you get the help you need. I know underneath the drugs and addiction, there's a sweet, beautiful, caring man fighting demons that are winning. Don't let them win, Gage. Fight harder and find happiness.
Xo, Sadie

IT'S BEEN OVER THREE MONTHS SINCE I'VE BEEN HOME. THE DAY OF THE FUNERAL, WHEN we buried three lifeless bodies, I walked out the door and haven't been back. As I stand on the front porch, staring at the door with the American flag wreath hanging from the Fourth of July, my heart races in my chest at the thought of walking through the door. I consider turning around and running away. I have my bank card, so I could stay in a hotel, but for how long?

At some point, I'll have to go inside and deal with everything I left behind, so with a deep, cleansing breath, I type in the code on the handle to unlock the door and then enter the alarm code to shut it off.

When I walk through the door, the sight in front of me causes me to choke up: trains… all over the floor. Collin loved trains and would play with them for hours. Too many times, Vincent would come home from work and step on them. A watery laugh bubbles up as I remember the way he would bounce from one foot to the other, swearing the trains to hell.

I switch on the light and am shocked when it actually works since I haven't paid a single bill in months. I walk farther into the house, taking in the toys and folded clothes. Vincent's loafers are in the corner. I stop by Collin's room first, and the second I turn on his light, waves of emotions nearly drown me. He hasn't stepped foot in his room in over three months, but I can still smell his shampoo. More trains are on the floor. I pad inside and find his favorite train on the bed along with his stuffed train the Easter Bunny brought him. Needing to feel close to him, I slide onto his bed and pull the stuffed train into my arms, dipping my face into the plush material and inhaling deeply.

Memories from the past several years flood back. Vincent and I getting married. Buying this home. Finding out I was pregnant. Collin's homecoming. Vincent admitting that he had a drug problem and promising to get help…

Tears roll down my face as I remember the good and the bad: Collin learning to walk and talk, and Vincent surprising us with a trip to Disney. Finding out my husband was still addicted to pills. Learning I was pregnant again. Vincent promising that he would never touch drugs again...

I have so many regrets, but they're all pointless because none of them will change my reality. My husband and son are dead. The baby growing in my belly is gone, and I'm all alone.

I spend the rest of the day in Collin's bed crying, telling myself I just need some time, and then I'll figure out my next move. As I close my eyes, his scent creating a warm blanket around me, the image of Gage pops into my head—the way he would lie behind me and hold me close—and I pray to whatever God that's up there that he gets his life together. I meant what I wrote to him: beneath the drugs and addiction is a sweet, caring, beautiful man. And if I were stronger, I would try to save him, but I just don't have it in me. I tried to save a man once from himself, and I learned the hard way that the only person who can save you is yourself. Which is what I'm going to do—save myself. Because I'm the only person I have left.

Seven

Gage

"GET UP!" THE BOOMING VOICE HAS ME SQUEEZING MY EYES AS I TRY TO BLOCK OUT THE hammering in my head.

"Gage, now!" Declan continues, determined to make my head explode.

"Get out of my room," I groan, reaching over so I can grab Sadie and get a good whiff of her sweet, floral scent. Only instead of finding her, my body rolls over and hits the ground, chin smacking the hardwood floor. "Fuck!"

"Serves you right. Now, get up."

I roll onto my back, prying my eyes open, and the first thing I notice is the fan. It's not the one in my room, but the one in the living room. *What the fuck…?*

I glance around and realize I'm not in my room but in the living room. *How the hell did I get out here?*

"Gage, where's Sadie?" Declan asks, snapping me from my thoughts.

"What?" I sit up and close my eyes when the pounding in my

head increases.

"Open your fucking eyes, bro."

I do what he says and find two women passed out: one on the loveseat and the other on the floor. And that's when everything comes back to me.

Braxton telling us he's moving in with Kaylee.

Declan asking if I'm moving Sadie in or if we're planning to get our own place.

Me freaking the hell out.

Going to Collided—the illegal underground club where I go when I want to get fucked up.

Bringing two women home.

Oh, fuck… Sadie.

I try to stand, but with the drugs still flowing through my veins, I stumble, crashing into the coffee table.

I faintly hear Declan calling my name, but I ignore him as I make a beeline straight to my room, which is empty. I check the balcony, but she's not there, so I try the bathroom. And that's where I see it… a note. I snatch it off the mirror and read the words.

She's gone.

She thanked me for saving her and then said goodbye.

The thought makes my stomach roil, and I drop to the toilet just in time to puke everything in my guts up.

"She leave?" Declan asks, his tone now cautious.

"Yeah," I choke out, grabbing a towel and wiping my mouth. "She's gone."

"Is there anything I can do?"

"Yeah, you can kick those women out," I tell him, my eyes going to the note on the floor.

Declan agrees and disappears, closing my door behind him.

Grabbing the note, I go back out to my bedroom and pull the

baggie out of my drawer, pouring the powder onto the nightstand. As I bring my nose to it, snorting two lines—the high is almost instant—I tell myself that Sadie's leaving is for the best. Then I pop a few pills as I try to convince myself that's the truth.

BEEP. BEEP. BEEP. BEEP.

"Gage, c'mon, man, you can do it. Wake up, please," Declan says, his voice raw with emotion. I wrench my lids open, and our eyes lock. "Oh, thank God." Tears fill his lids, his worried features making him look like he's aged ten years, and my stomach knots, trying to remember how I ended up in the hospital with my friend and roommate sitting next to me and begging me to wake up.

"What happened?" I croak out when I come up with nothing.

"You overdosed. I found you half dead in your room. Kendall called for an ambulance, and they were able to save you." He exhales a harsh breath as I take in the dark circles under his eyes and the way his brow is furrowed in stress. I did this to him. I caused him stress because I can't deal with my shit.

"Gage," Declan says softly. "I have to ask… Did you try to kill yourself?"

His words, his question, triggers a memory…

"Hey, Tor." I stumble over to her grave and drop onto the ground. "Looks like it's just you and me today." I glance over at the three gravestones that have been without company every day since Sadie took off. The first few times I stopped by, I told myself I was visiting Tori. But when Sadie never showed up, and the manager said he hadn't seen her, I started to get worried that something had happened to her. So I kept

showing up, hoping to run into her. I told myself that once I saw she was okay, I would stop. Only she never, not once, showed up.

The last day I was there, the couple I met before showed up...

"I was wondering if you've seen Sadie," I ask, trying to sound as casual as possible.

The woman smiles sadly. "She actually moved away a couple of months ago. Said it was too hard to be here... with the memories and all." She places a small bouquet into each of the holders. "Sadie asked that we come once a month and bring flowers since she's too far away to come herself."

"We talk to her occasionally," the gentleman says. "Would you like us to tell her anything?"

I shake my head as it hits me. I failed my mom and couldn't save Tori. Then I drove Sadie away.

"Yeah," I admit to Declan. "I did. I tried to kill myself."

They're the hardest words I've ever spoken, but they're also the most honest, and I owe him that—fuck, I owe all the guys that. After I left the cemetery, I was low... so fucking low. I was missing my mom and Tori... and Sadie. Fuck, I was missing Sadie so fucking much. Her touch and her scent and the way she just made everything more bearable. And I couldn't take it anymore. The pain in my heart just became too much. And I wanted it all to end. I wasn't thinking clearly and just needed a moment of reprieve.

"Dec," I choke out. "My heart... it fucking hurts."

Declan nods in understanding. "We're going to get you help, Gage. We should've gotten you help sooner, but we fucked up. We thought you just needed time, but we were wrong. I promise you..." He takes my hand in his. "We're going to get you the best fucking help."

"Damn right, we are," Camden says, walking in with Easton and Braxton. "We never should've let you get this bad." Camden leans over and kisses the top of my head, and tears fill my eyes. I don't deserve these guys. They've always been there for me, and in return, what do I do? Put them in the worst position possible.

"This isn't on you guys. It's on me," I tell them, needing to take responsibility. I fucked up. I let the drugs overtake my life. Instead of dealing with my shit, I chose to escape it, which not only hurt me but also hurt everyone around me.

"It is on you," Easton agrees. "But you're family, and we should've intervened sooner. We have everything set up. It's a ninety-day program, but once they evaluate you, they'll alter the plan to your needs."

Ninety days... Fuck. "What about the band?" We haven't recorded shit in months because I was too busy spiraling.

"It'll be here when you're better," Camden says.

"I can't ask you guys to put your lives on hold for me." They've been here for me for years, and all I've done is held them back every step of the way. I can't keep doing this to them. And what if I can't get better?

I glance down at my hands, which are shaking with need. Already craving the high. Even as we're discussing me getting help, I'm thinking about the drugs, the escape.

"You're not asking us to do anything," Declan says. "We're a band. The four of us. And unless we're all in this together, we're not doing shit."

I open my mouth to argue, but Easton speaks up before I can. "This is Roy." He points at a gentleman I didn't notice was standing in the corner until now. "He'll hang out here until you're cleared by the doctor to leave." In other words, they're worried I might try to kill myself again, so they're making sure I'm not alone and given the opportunity.

I nod toward the man, who smiles sympathetically.

"And this is Bernadine Winters," Easton says when an older woman walks through the door, a warm smile on her face. She's accompanied by another woman, who's a bit younger and has a more serious expression. "She's from Changing Seasons, the private facility you'll be going to."

"Good morning," Bernadine says, stepping over to me and extending her hand to shake mine. "As Mr. Blackwood mentioned, I'm Bernadine Winters, and this is Pamela Finn, our resident psychiatrist who's been assigned to you. To get started, we have some questions we need to go over and paperwork that needs to be filled out. Are you up for that, Mr. Sharp?"

"Yes," I tell her, ignoring the way my heart races in my chest because I'm craving the high I'm not getting at the moment. "I'm up for that."

After going over my situation with Bernadine and Pamela, I sign the papers, agreeing to voluntarily check myself into Changing Seasons mental health and drug rehab facility. They also go over the papers Easton's wife, Sophia, had them sign, such as NDAs and all the necessary shit to cover my ass. Once all the legalities are out of the way, I'm monitored for the next several days while the doctors ensure my overdose didn't create any issues with my kidneys, brain, liver, and heart. The cravings worsen, and thankfully, I'm given something to help curb them.

The day I'm cleared and discharged, my friends are there to see me off. With tears in their eyes, they hug and tell me they're rooting for me. But it's hard to look any of them in the eye, knowing I'm the reason for their stress. Without the drugs to fog my brain, the guilt I feel is stronger, more potent. They should be making music and enjoying their families, not dealing with my shit and my fuckups. And then a thought hits me, something Sadie mentioned when she was talking to me about her late husband. What if I get cleaned up, only to relapse? He swore several times he was pill-free when he wasn't. The thought of letting the guys down is too much, the weight nearly bringing me to my metaphorical knees.

"What's going through your head?" Pamela asks as we get into the Town Car.

I shake my head, and she frowns. "In order to help you, you're going to have to be honest with me. Otherwise, everything we're doing is pointless. So I'm going to ask you again. What's going through your head?"

"I'm afraid of letting them down." I nod toward my mini entourage of people watching us take off. So the paparazzi couldn't catch a glimpse of me, I was taken out through a private underground exit. "I'm afraid of failing them. I've failed so many damn people in my life," I admit. "I don't think I can handle failing them too... I mean, fuck, I already have, I guess." I think about my next words for a moment before I continue. "Can I make a request?"

"Sure," she says. "Can't be sure I can oblige, but you can always make a request."

"Aside from Easton being told I'm okay, I think it'd be best if nobody was able to call or visit." That way, they can move on the best they can. And if I fail them... I won't have to hear the disappointment in their voices... see it in their eyes.

Eight

Sadie

"JESUS EFFING CHRIST!" I THROW MY ARMS AROUND THE PORCELAIN BOWL, RETCHING into it as I curse bacon to hell. I love bacon and could eat it with everything. It's one of those foods that makes everything better. Mac 'n' cheese—yummy—but add bacon, and it's amazing. An egg and cheese sandwich is delicious, but add bacon, and it's perfection.

Bacon has only been my nemesis two times in my life—when I was pregnant. I've been avoiding it since the first time I threw up a few weeks ago and assumed I caught a bug, only for it not to go away after several days. But it's time I face the facts… During the deepest and darkest days of my grieving, I didn't think about birth control. It was irresponsible and stupid, but I just didn't have it in me to think logically. My only focus was getting through each day and praying for there to eventually be a light at the end of the tunnel.

Gage was obviously too high to think about it, and he probably assumed I was on something. He never asked, and it never crossed my mind…until now.

Once I'm almost positive I'm done throwing up, I wash out my mouth and brush my teeth, then head back into the kitchen to make a bacon-less egg and cheese sandwich. I'm mixing the eggs when something on the television catches my attention.

"In our dirt of the day, our sources have confirmed that Raging Chaos's drummer, Gage Sharp, has been discharged from New York Medical after a recent overdose that our sources say was an attempt at ending his life…"

I rush over to the television to hear what she's saying, but she's already moved on to her next bit of gossip. Could it be? No, there's no way. There are a million Gages out there, right? What are the chances that…?

Grabbing my phone, I click on the internet and search Gage Sharp, then click on the images, and sure enough, the gorgeous face of the man I spent almost three months with pops up. It's been over three months since I've seen him, but the moment my eyes land on his curly brown hair, broody blue eyes, that strong jawline, and the single brow—that's sporting a simple bar through it—quirked up, silently telling the world to fuck off, my belly does a quick flip-flop.

I drop onto the couch—my food forgotten—and spend hours learning everything I can about the mysterious man who carried me out of the cemetery and, in his own way, took care of me for months. Once I'm done, everything suddenly makes sense: the nice apartment, him not working, his roommates…Gage Sharp is the drummer for Raging Chaos, one of the world's hottest rock bands… and he's also a drug addict.

My hand instinctually goes to my belly, knowing what I have to do. If what the news is saying is true, then Gage not only overdosed on drugs but he also did it with the intent of ending his life. I pray to God that he's okay and gets the help he needs, but I will do everything in my power to keep the little miracle growing inside me safe, including making sure Gage never finds out. I already lost two babies and a husband to drugs, and there's no way I'm going to let that happen again. I didn't protect my babies the way I should have last time, but I won't ever make that mistake again.

Nine

Gage

BREAKFAST. GROUP THERAPY. WORK OUT. FREE TIME. LUNCH. INDIVIDUAL THERAPY. MUSIC. Free time. Dinner. Free time…

My life has become a routine of wash, rinse, repeat, but it's not a bad thing. I know what to expect, thrive on the structure and stability, and even revel in it. I haven't done a single drug in months, and my body recognizes that it's better because of it. But my brain… fuck, it still craves the high every goddamn day.

"I'm not ready," I tell Pamela, the woman who's been by my side every step of the way. From the first few weeks of hell during detox to the months I've spent trying to analyze every part of my life so I can go back into the real world and function like a normal adult. Only I feel like one of those animals who've been injured and saved, spent months getting rehabilitated, but because they've spent so much time there, they've become domesticated and wouldn't be able to survive in the wild.

"Why don't you believe you're ready?"

"Because I did drugs for six years, and I've only been drug-free for three months." The thought of going back into the wild scares the shit out of me and makes my heart race in my chest. We've been talking several times a day every day this week to help prepare me, but it's not fucking helping. I've had three anxiety attacks and had to be hospitalized because I thought I was having a heart attack.

"Gage, do you think it's possible you're scared because you've refused to speak to anyone outside of these walls? You're afraid of stepping back into a life you've only known while high?"

"Yeah," I agree, the lump in my throat forming. "That, and failing my friends, and then turning to drugs and then ending up right back here. I'm not ready."

I clutch my chest as it rises and falls in quick succession, feeling the stirrings of another anxiety attack. "What if I'm not the same guy they know? What if I can't play the drums and the band fails? What if I can play, and then we go on tour, and I'm back to craving the drugs?" I voice my concerns, the same ones I've expressed all week. "What if I walk out of here and I can't handle it? What if I go to the grave to see Tori, and the pain in my heart hurts so bad that I'm not strong enough to say no?"

Pamela opens her mouth to speak, but I cut her off. "And before you say that's what my sponsor's for, what if he's not there? What if I don't call him because I want to do the drugs?"

With every *what-if*, my heart pumps harder, my palms clutch tighter. Sweat beads across my forehead. "I'm scared," I tell her, not for the first time. "I can't fail them again. They're waiting for me to go back to making music and being their friend, and I'm fucking scared. Please," I beg. "I'm not ready. I need to stay longer."

She releases a soft sigh and nods in understanding, and I instantly calm. "Okay, here's what we're going to do…"

Ten

Gage
SEVEN MONTHS LATER

AS I RUN DOWN THE SANDY BEACH, THE CHILLY SALT WATER LAPS AGAINST MY ANKLES AS the wind whips around my face. It's November in Long Beach, so it's cold as fuck outside, but that doesn't stop me from going on my morning run. The cold air fills my lungs, reminding me that I'm alive.

When I arrived at the beach house after being discharged from Changing Seasons, I spent hours at the beach. Swimming in the ocean, watching the stars at night. Writing lyrics. Finding myself.

With my sponsor, Gabe, by my side, and Pamela doing sessions via video, it felt like I was taking baby steps. Not quite in the wild but not caged either. I hate that aside from a couple of texts, I haven't spoken to anyone, but I needed to focus on my healing. While on drugs, I didn't like the person I was, but without them, I didn't know who the hell I was. And I needed to figure that out on my own. Who I am without the band, without my friends. Without the ghosts of my mom and Tori hanging over my head. I'm still not quite there, but at ten months drug-free, I feel a hell of a lot closer.

A month ago, Gabe moved out, and we now talk daily on the phone. My calls with Pamela are also down to every other day. See… baby steps. Our last conversation was about if I've decided when I'm returning home… *if* I'm returning home. Pamela pointed out that I'm not the same person I was six years ago, and if being in a band is no longer what I'm interested in, the guys will understand.

But I'm not ready to give up the band just yet. And not because they've been waiting for me, but because before the drugs, I loved beating on those fucking drums, and I want a chance to see if I still love them. The only problem is, there's only one way to find out… I have to go home.

And I'm a fucking chickenshit.

I'm slowing to a light jog as I get closer to the house when I spot a woman leaning against the fence. She's wrapped up in a winter coat with a beanie on her head as she rubs her gloved hands together.

"Are you freaking crazy?" Kendall, Declan's wife and mother of his five-week-old twins, yells as I approach. "It's like thirty degrees out here."

She smiles warmly at me, and I pull her into a hug, realizing this is the first human contact I've had in months. "You look so good, Gage," she murmurs, kissing my cheek.

"Thank you. How are the babies?" I ask as we walk up to the house to get out of the cold. I was shocked to learn that Declan—after all the years of crushing on Kendall—finally got the girl. I was also so damn happy for him.

"Perfect. Amazing. Exhausting," she says with a laugh.

"They with you?"

She shakes her head. "I thought it would be best if I came alone."

When she texted me a couple of days ago, telling me that she got my number from Declan and he didn't know she was contacting me, she asked if she could come and see me.

"It's beautiful here," she says, staring out at the ocean. "I can see why you love it."

"I'm hiding," I admit. After she contacted me, I spoke to Pamela, and even without her saying it, I knew it was time to go home. "I needed more time, but I'm ready to go back."

I glance at her, and she smiles softly at me. "I thought you were going to make this hard on me. I even brought in the big guns." She nods behind me, and when I look back, I find Kaylee standing there with glassy eyes.

"Come here, you." I open my arms, and she rushes into my embrace. Over the years, since Tori died, we've remained in touch, despite her and Braxton parting ways for a while. And last year when we went on tour, and they reconnected, we grew close. Tori was her best friend, and she missed her like I did... like I do.

"I heard you got married." Despite not texting or talking to anyone, they continued to send me pictures and messages to keep me updated. They were what kept me going during the hard days, knowing they were living their best life, happy and finding love.

"We did," she gushes, hugging me tighter. "I miss you, Gage. We all do."

"I miss you guys too. I'm sorry it's taken me so long."

"No, no apologizing. We're just so happy to see you healthy. You look so good." Kaylee squeezes my bicep playfully. "And you're all muscular."

I laugh. "Yeah, well, when I'm not spending my days getting high or playing music, I have a lot of time on my hands."

"Speaking of which," Kendall says. "Are you... planning to play music again?" I can hear it in her voice, the concern. Not for me, though. For her husband. He's the reason she's here. Because I've been gone for so long, and the band has refused to play a single chord or sing a single lyric without me.

"I'm going to try," I tell her truthfully. "I can't promise anything, but I'm going to come home and take it one day at a time."

She smiles and nods. "Thank you. The guys have missed you so much."

We hang out for a bit longer and chat, the girls catching me up on everyone, and then they take off after I assure them that I'll be home for Thanksgiving.

I spend the day packing and getting my shit together. Since the apartment's no longer available, I agree to stay with Kaylee and Braxton while I figure out my next move.

Two days later, I arrive at the Blackwoods for Thanksgiving. When I walk through the door, I'm met with hugs and warm greetings. I thank everyone, but notice Declan is nowhere to be found.

"He fell asleep on the couch," Kendall says.

"Give me a few minutes," I tell everyone, needing some time with my friend. I'm close with all the guys, but Declan and I have always had a different connection. Maybe it was because Braxton and Camden found the women they wanted to spend their lives with, leaving Declan and me to bachelor it out together—him with his woman out of reach, and mine... well, she was also out of my reach.

The day I woke up in the hospital and saw the look in his eyes, then learned he's the reason I'm still alive, I'd never felt like more of a failure in my life. Had I not made it, he would've had to live with that guilt, and I promised myself I would never put someone I love in that position again.

"Am I dreaming?" Declan asks, his eyes fluttering open.

"As sweet as it is that you apparently dream about me..." I chuckle. "Nah, it's me, in the flesh."

"Where's everyone?" he asks, glancing around.

"Giving us a minute." I sit on the couch next to him. "I wanted to say I'm sorry. I shouldn't have stayed gone as long as I did, but I needed the time."

"What made you come back?"

"Your wife." I smile at him. "Congrats, by the way. Finally got the girl."

"Kendall?"

"Yeah, she came and saw me. Told me it was time to come home."

He smiles softly. "So where've you been? Why'd you stay away for so long?"

I drop back against the couch and turn my head to face him. "Where do I even begin?"

"How about at the beginning?"

And so, I do... I spend the next hour telling everyone where I've been and the journey I've been on to get here. Admitting that while I'm drug-free, I'm still scared as hell and unsure if I'll be able to play again, let alone tour.

When I'm done, Declan puts his hand on my shoulder and says, "All that matters is that you're here."

"Agreed," Braxton adds. "If the band doesn't ever play another song again, we don't give a fuck as long as you're healthy. You are all that matters."

"We're so damn glad to have you back," Camden says, hugging me. "The holidays wouldn't have been the same without you."

Every doubt I had about coming home evaporates as I glance around, taking in their words. I'm where I belong... with my family.

Eleven

Gage
THREE MONTHS LATER

"YOU KNOW WHAT YOU NEED?" KAYLEE ASKS AS I STROLL INTO THE CONDO, DRIPPING IN sweat from my morning run.

"No, but I'm sure you're going to tell me."

She ignores my sarcasm and hands me a bottle of water. Taking it, I give her a grateful smile and chug half of it down.

"To go out on a date."

I choke on the liquid, and she laughs, making me glare her way. "The last thing I need is to go on a date. A part of my program is—"

"Staying away from relationships," she finishes, rolling her eyes. "Yeah, I know, but that's only for a year, and it's been over a year now. There's nothing wrong with putting yourself out there. When's the last time you were with anyone?"

My thoughts go straight to Sadie. Her bleeding heart and broken soul. She was destroyed and damaged but still so strong. Strong enough to walk away from me after I did the worst thing I could do: push her away.

NIKKI ASH

It was for the best because she deserved more than I could give her back then. Had she stayed, I might've brought her down with me. But that hasn't stopped me from thinking about her over the past year and a half. Once I was drug-free and could think straight, I spoke to Pamela about her, about the guilt I felt for what I did to her.

She asked if I wanted to reach out and apologize, but I didn't want to put her in that position, so instead, I had Easton do it for me. I told him to just make sure wherever she was, she was safe and taken care of. I didn't want to know anything except that she wasn't on the streets somewhere, and if she was, to make sure to get her off them. He got back to me a week later and said she moved to Virginia, was renting a home in a nice subdivision, and she looked good. Not happy, but okay.

"Gage?" Kaylee says, knocking me out of my thoughts. "It's okay to find happiness."

Her words take me back to the past, to Declan saying the same shit about Sadie. In another lifetime, I would've scooped her up and held her close, keeping her for myself. But I wasn't capable of handling a woman like her with care. I think Kaylee and Declan are right… It's time for me to find some happiness. But right now, the only thing I want to focus on is the band. The guys have had my back, and it's my turn to have theirs.

"I know," I tell her. "And it'll happen when the time is right, but right now, the only happiness I'm after comes in the form of a drum kit." I give her a wink and stalk off to take a shower. Today is the first day the guys and I are back in the studio writing. If all goes well, we'll have our songs finalized in the next couple of weeks and then start recording. Our goal is to release the album this winter and tour next summer.

After taking a shower, I tell Braxton I'll see him at the studio and

98

then go by the cemetery. I haven't been here since the day I OD'd, but with Sadie fresh on my mind, I figure it's time. Since it's been a while, I pick up flowers on my way for Tori, and at the last second, I grab two more small bouquets for Sadie's babies. With her living in Virginia, I imagine she isn't able to visit them the way she did during our time together.

After placing them into each of their holders, I have a seat in front of Tori. I can't believe it's been almost eight years. It's crazy how fast time flies. One minute, I was kissing her at the beach, and the next, I was so low I almost ended my life.

"This is the first time I've visited you sober," I say, hoping wherever she is, she can hear me. "I was lost for a while. The guilt over the way your life ended consumed me. But I know now that what happened wasn't my fault. It was that piece of shit's and your mother's, and I'll never forgive either of them."

I run my fingers through the grass, tugging on a few strands absentmindedly as I gather my thoughts. "While I was in rehab, I thought a lot about you. About children and teenagers in the same situation as you. Scared and feeling like they're alone in the world. For the past several years, instead of honoring your life, trying to right the wrong, I drowned in the injustice of the situation. But that's going to change.

"I'm starting a foundation called Tori's Angels, and it's going to help children and teens in the same situation as you have someone they can go to who will listen. I know now why you didn't tell me. I was too close to you, and you feared for what would happen to me, but had you had someone on the outside you could've gone to..." I choke up, my emotions getting the better of me. "Things could've been different."

Instead of leaving to go to the studio, I spend some time with Tori, catching her up on how everyone's doing—Cam and Layla are in parental bliss with Felix, their six-year-old, and Marianna, their one-and-a-half-year-old. Braxton and Kaylee are still in that honeymoon stage, where they're fucking like jackrabbits every night, which reminds me—I need to start looking for my own place. If I have to hear Kaylee scream Braxton's name much longer, my ears might permanently bleed. And Declan and Kendall are so much in love that it's sickening to watch. Luckily, they're so busy with their six-month-old twins, Morgan and Nina, they don't have time to fuck like Kaylee and Braxton.

As I tell her about them, I can't help the way my heart swells in my chest, wishing I could have what they have. They've found love and family and aren't alone. I've craved to have all of that my entire life, and now that I'm sober and ready to move forward, I hope to find that one day.

When we're all caught up, I tell her I'll visit again soon and then take off to meet up with the guys. I'm both excited and nervous to be back. It's been years since I've done this sober, and I'd be lying if I didn't admit to being concerned. Luckily, I have my sponsor, Gabe, in case I feel the need to get high, and I'm planning to go to a meeting later today if we get done early enough—if not, I'll go to one tomorrow.

The second I step foot through Blackwood Records' doors, I'm met with Easton and Sophia standing by the front desk.

When she sees me, she comes straight for me, enveloping me in her warm embrace. She's always been the closest thing to a mother figure I've had, and since I've returned, she's been around a lot. She admitted to feeling guilty for not stepping up and forcing me to get help—not realizing just how bad it was—but I told her the same thing I told the guys and their wives. Nobody could've forced me to do shit. I had to hit rock bottom. And once I did, once I came too damn close to ending my life, I was ready to handle my shit and stand on my own two feet. And I'll be damned if I ever fall again.

"You look amazing," Sophia says, kissing my cheek. "Every time I see you, I swear you look even better, healthier. How could we not see it before?" She shakes her head, liquid filling her eyes. "I'll never forgive—"

"Stop," I say gently. "The only thing that matters is that I'm okay. Everyone having my back and being here… means the world to me." I look her in the eyes. "You guys are my family."

Before she can get even sappier, Easton speaks up. "The guys are already in the studio." He gives me a quick hug and pats my back. "Welcome back, son."

My heart races behind my rib cage as I walk into the studio where the guys are. This will be the first time in years that I'm writing, playing, and recording sober. One of my biggest fears is that the music will bring me back to my darkest days and have me craving the high. Then there's the fear that I won't be able to play the same, that being sober will fuck up the vibe, and I'll let the guys down.

Thankfully, the guys don't make a big deal about me being here. Camden tosses a water bottle my way, Braxton throws me a chin jut, and Declan smiles softly. And then we get started on our next album.

The days turn into weeks, and before we know it, we have enough songs to create an album. Everyone has their own way of doing shit, but for us, we'll spend anywhere from a few weeks to a couple of months practicing, recording, tweaking, and then finalizing every song. Then begins the other shit: photo shoots, the artwork, merch designs, deciding which songs will be the single, promoting the upcoming album, planning the tour, and the list goes on.

"I think we should start with 'Deep,'" Camden says, referring to one of the songs I wrote while in rehab. "It's emotional as hell, and my dad thinks we should consider it for the single."

"Sounds good," Braxton says, grabbing his guitar.

"I'm down," Declan agrees.

Slowly, I walk over to the drums, immediately recognizing them as my own and not the studio's.

"We figured you'd want your own," Camden says, sounding unsure.

"Thanks," I mutter.

Pulling my sticks out of my back pocket, I sit behind my kit and take a moment to get a feel for them. It's been a long-ass time since I've played, but the moment my foot presses the pedal and my sticks hit the drums, it feels as though the broken parts of me have been sewn together. I'm not perfect—never will be—but as we come together as a band for the first time in almost two years, I feel whole again.

"Fuck yes," Camden says when the song comes to a close. "This is going to be one helluva comeback album."

His words hit in the pit of my stomach. Had I not fucked up, there wouldn't need to be a damn comeback album.

As if the guys know exactly what I'm thinking, Declan says, "Don't go there. We all needed this break. Camden was busy having kids, and Braxton and I both got married. Kendall and I had twins. I would've wanted time at home with them anyway. We'd been hitting it hard for years, and all of us needed a break. This isn't on you."

Knowing they'll only argue if I point out that an almost two-year break wasn't what anyone intended, I simply nod, once again thankful that my friends have my back. They might not blame me, but I blame myself, and I'll do everything in my power to make sure this next album is the best one yet.

We're about to take it from the top when my phone goes off with a text from Kaylee: **When's the last time you spoke to Sadie?**

Me: Not since shit ended between us... Why?

I never told anyone what went down between us. Declan kind of knows since he was there the morning after—and I'm sure he's smart enough to put the pieces together—but he's never brought it up, and I know he wouldn't talk about it with anyone.

A picture comes through, along with a question: **Is this her?**

I zoom in on it and find myself staring at a smiling Sadie. Her red hair is up in a messy bun, and her eyes are bright, filled with happiness. My heart lurches in my chest at how much I've missed her. Even being as fucked up as I was back then, she still crawled into the crevices of my broken self and embedded herself under my skin. In the short time we spent together, I was reminded of what it was like to have someone to talk to, to share shit with. Most days were bad, so fucking bad, but some days were good.

I close my eyes, recalling how she would look at me and smile every once in a while. It was a sad as fuck smile but still filled with hope and promises of tomorrow. At the time, I wasn't capable of either one, but she was, and seeing how happy she looks now… While I hate the way I hurt her, I know I did the right thing for her.

Another picture comes through, this one of her with her head thrown back in a laugh. *Fuck, she's beautiful.* What I wouldn't give to hear her laughing. She will forever be the woman who got away.

Just as I'm about to confirm that the woman in the pictures is, in fact, Sadie, a third picture comes through that has me freezing in place. A little girl with curly red hair. She's standing next to Sadie, both of them smiling, as Sadie points at something in the distance. The little girl can't be more than a year old, which doesn't make sense since Sadie lost her son, unborn daughter, and husband, leaving her with no one.

"What's going on?" Declan asks.

"How old does she look to you?" I show him the picture.

"Is that Sadie?"

"Yeah. How old is the little girl?"

Camden walks over and glances over my shoulder. "Maybe ten months old, give or take…"

I do the math in my head. The number of months she'd have been pregnant. How long it's been since I've last seen her… That would make the baby roughly eight months. It's possible she met someone after me, but there's also the possibility that—

"Oh, shit," Declan murmurs, speaking my thought out loud. "Is she yours?"

I try to remember if we used protection, but I can't recall ever doing so. I never thought about condoms or if she was on birth control. I was too busy chasing my next high and getting lost in her.

"I don't know," I tell him, "but I'm about to find out."

Twelve

Sadie

TODAY IS VINCENT'S BIRTHDAY—HE WOULD'VE BEEN THIRTY-TWO YEARS OLD. IT'S BEEN eighteen months since I've visited my family. When I decided to move to Virginia to start fresh, I never planned to stay away as long as I did. But then I found out I was pregnant and then gave birth, and with every step forward, I couldn't bring myself to go backward... back to the cemetery where my family was buried, back to the heartache I endured. Back to where I left Gage and the jagged pieces of what was left of my heart.

Little by little, with every smile, every laugh, my daughter has helped bring life back to the vital organ in my chest, so I continued to move forward... for her... for us. It's not that I haven't thought about my family. I show her pictures of Collin every day, explain that he's her brother in heaven. She doesn't understand, but one day she will. She'll know that in the midst of all the chaos, she was the calm in my storm. That because of her, I was able to breathe again, *live* again. And so, I stayed away, not wanting to risk falling back down that hole filled with depression.

Until now.

Vincent's mom called and begged me to visit. She hasn't seen me since I left and would like to meet my daughter. When they found out about her, they were confused and upset, but over time, they became supportive. They aren't her grandparents, but they send her gifts and video chat with her as if they are. They love me like their own daughter and, by default, love my little girl as well.

Amidst the dark, my little girl brought light to all of us.

"All right, my little cherry pie." I lift my daughter into my arms and blow a raspberry into her neck, making her giggle. "It's time to get going."

"Ma, Ma, Ma." She shakes her head, trying to wiggle out of my arms. She's only recently started babbling what sounds like Mama, and I swear every time she does it, I want to give her the world. We've spent the morning at A Latte Fun, an indoor playground for kids. I'm hoping to wear her out so when we go to the cemetery, she'll sleep through it. I'm unsure of how being there will hit me, and the last thing I want is for her to see me crying.

"We have to go," I tell her, holding her tighter as I walk us toward the door so I can change her diaper and get our shoes on. "We'll come back again." After changing her diaper, I set her on the cushioned seat and hand her a sippy cup so she can get something to drink while I get her shoes on. Once she's ready to go, I open the stroller and buckle her in, then get my shoes on.

As I'm pushing the stroller out the door, I pull out my phone to let my in-laws know I'm on my way and will meet them at the cemetery when the stroller gets stuck on something. I set the phone into the cup holder and am preparing to get it over whatever hump it's caught on, but when I look up, I realize it's not stuck on anything. It's been stopped... by Gage.

Fuck.

He raises a single brow, the brow with a metal bar going through it from top to bottom, and his eyes pierce into mine. I stumble back slightly, taken aback. I don't remember a lot from our short time together, but I could never forget his eyes, the way they were dimmed and lifeless. Only now, they're bright and filled with life and… hurt… hurt with a mixture of hardness to them, and I know in my gut, somehow, he *knows*.

My thoughts are confirmed when his gaze descends, landing on my daughter. His eyes soften as he takes her in. She's completely unaware of what's happening, babbling away and slamming her pacifier against the tray while she scoops up Cheerios with her other hand.

"Is she—?"

His words are cut off by a woman trying to get by. "Excuse me," she says, annoyance laced in her tone, and it's then I realize we're still standing in the middle of the doorway.

"I'm sorry," I tell her.

Gage backs up, and I push the stroller through, exiting onto the busy sidewalk. People in a rush skate around us as I move to the side before someone trips over the stroller.

I can feel Gage's eyes on me the entire time, watching, assessing. It's been a year and a half since I've seen him, and while he looks like the same man I walked out on, he also looks different. Healthier. But that's always the case with addicts, right? They're up, and then they're down… I saw it over and over again with Vincent. He would be up, on top of the world, making promises, and then he would fall, taking all those promises with him. Until the last time, when he not only took all his promises but also our son with him.

The thought has me needing to get as far away from Gage as possible. Away from his addiction. His ups and downs. But before I can make my escape, he's stepping in front of the stroller, putting his hand on the handlebar and blocking me in.

"Is she mine?" he asks, cutting straight to the chase, his eyes locking with mine.

"She's mine." I jut my chin out in defiance. "Now, if you'd please move, I have somewhere I need to be."

Only he doesn't move. He stands there, in my way, his gaze flitting between my daughter and me. "I know she's yours," he finally says. "She has your beautiful red hair and fair skin. That's not what I asked. Is. She. Mine?"

I know what he asked… what he's asking. But I can't bring myself to say what he needs me to say. It's my job to protect her, to keep her safe, and I can't do that if he has access to her. I already failed my son. I can't fail my daughter too. So despite Gage already knowing the answer, I say the only thing I can say. The only words that will come out of my mouth. The only answer that will protect my little girl, keep her out of harm's way, and ensure that her fate isn't the same as my son's—her lifeless body buried six feet under because I trusted an addict who made promises he couldn't keep.

"She's mine and only mine," I tell him as I pry his fingers from the stroller's handlebar.

"Sadie," he growls, refusing to let me go. "She has my blue eyes and curly hair. Are you going to deny that she's mine?"

"Don't do this. Please, Gage," I choke out, my emotions getting the better of me. "Please don't do this. I… I have to protect her. She's my entire world. Please, let me walk away. Whatever you think you know, just… for her sake, let it go… Let us go."

Gage's eyes widen, and he steps closer to me. "You want me to forget that I have a daughter? A daughter you didn't tell me about? Are you serious right now?"

"Yes… Yes, I'm serious. You're… an addict," I hiss, trying like hell to remain strong. "Do you not remember how she was conceived?

What happened *after* she was conceived? I'm trying to protect Rory, and I can't do that with you coming around. So please—"

"Rory?" he asks.

"What?"

"You said Rory. Is that her name?" His face softens as he glances down at her.

"It's what I call her, but her name is Aurora. The name means dawn, like a new day. And that's what she is for me: a new day, a fresh beginning," I choke out, tears filling my lids. "Gage, please." I place my hand on his chest. "She's taken care of and loved and… safe. Please don't do this. Don't ask to be a part of her life and risk hurting her."

Up until now, Rory has been quiet, munching away on her Cheerios and distracted by the passersby, but she must've had enough because she screeches, blubbering out, "Ma, Ma, Ma," grabbing both Gage's and my attention.

With the heat of his stare on me, I reach down and unbuckle her, pulling her into my arms. Her head goes to my shoulder, silently indicating that she's tired and ready for a nap. "I already buried two babies," I tell him. "One because a man couldn't stay away from drugs. I can't do that again. I'm not asking you for anything. I haven't asked for a penny. I just want to love her and keep her safe." I lay a soft kiss to the back of her head, inhaling her sweet baby scent. "Please. Do the right thing and let me go… let *us* go."

Gage's eyes redden slightly, filled with unshed tears, and I hate myself for asking him to walk away from his daughter, but I have to put my daughter first. I have to protect her at all costs, even if that means keeping her from the man who helped create her.

When he doesn't say anything back, I take that as my answer, and before he can change his mind, I grab the stroller with one hand and push it back onto the sidewalk, needing to get away from him as quick as possible.

I don't look back, don't stop until I get to the train station, and the entire time, I don't think about the guilt trying to catch up with me. I refuse to feel guilty for protecting my daughter. I'm doing what's best for her, keeping her safe. That's what a mother does, and that's what I'll always do until my last breath. I might not have been able to do that for Collin and wasn't given the chance to do that for Rebekah, but I will succeed with Rory. At least Gage didn't argue with me about it. Despite knowing she's half his, he let me go. He heard my pleas and did what was best for her—let us go.

"Oh, Sadie," Janice says when we walk up, pulling me into a hug. "It's so good to see you." She kisses my cheek, then looks down at Rory, who's back in her stroller fast asleep. "I know this is hard for you, but thank you for coming."

We walk over to the three graves, and seeing my babies' names hits me straight in the heart. I'll always grieve for Vincent, but over the years, my sadness for him has turned into anger. He's the reason our little boy died. He put his habit before Collin and took him down with him. Now, he's not here to mourn the loss of our son or feel the pain I feel every day. I would never express my feelings to Janice and Henry since he's their son, and it's not their fault he had a drug problem, but it doesn't stop me from feeling the way I do.

"It seems someone left flowers," Janie says when she goes to put small bouquets into the holders. Vincent's is the only one empty, so she places one bouquet into his. "Did you already come by?" she asks.

"No." I glance over at the nearby grave where Gage visited and notice the same flowers there as in my babies' holders. It's too much of a coincidence… It had to be Gage. He knows I haven't been here, so he left flowers for my babies. The thought has me pressing my hand to my chest and rubbing at the ache forming there.

We spend some time at the graves. Janice reminisces about Vincent, noting only the good memories she has of her son. I join in occasionally, but mostly leave her to it, knowing she really just needs us to be here with her. Vincent was their only child, and the day they lost him, like me, they lost their entire world.

When she's all cried out, she wipes her eyes and asks if I'd like to join them for dinner. I'm about to take her up on it when the sound of the footsteps crunching on the grass catches my attention, and my eyes meet Gage's.

"I'd like to spend a little longer here, if that's okay," I tell her. "Maybe we can meet for breakfast tomorrow? We don't leave until the afternoon."

She eyes Gage curiously but nods. "That would be great. I'd love to spend some time with Aurora when she's awake."

With a kiss and a hug from each of them, they head down the sidewalk, leaving Gage and me alone.

"We have to stop meeting like this," he says.

"Like what?" I ask, confused.

"You know…" He nods toward the graves. "At a cemetery."

"You left flowers." I don't have to explain what I'm referring to—he already knows.

"I did. Yesterday. Those people who were with you mentioned you moved away, so when I returned, after being gone for the past year, and came to visit Tori, I brought your babies flowers too."

"You were gone for over a year?" After it was in the news that he overdosed, trying to take his life, he pretty much dropped off the face of the planet.

"Yeah, I was in rehab," he confirms, "and then spent some time away… after I tried to kill myself."

"I'm glad you're… okay."

He steps toward me. "I'm more than okay. I'm sober and drug-free. Haven't touched anything in fourteen months." He glances down at a still sleeping Rory and smiles softly. "I fucked up so damn badly with you, and I am so sorry. I was at my lowest…" He shakes his head. "I can't take back what I did, and I never intended on contacting you because I know I hurt you, but then Kaylee texted me a picture of you and our little girl and…"

"She's mine," I repeat. "Not yours, *mine*. I don't care about you fucking up. I knew you were an addict when I met you, but I was grieving. I will forever be grateful to you for taking me in when I was grieving and needed a safe place to stay and giving me Aurora. But what we had…" I choke out. "It was nothing more than two fucked-up, broken people getting lost in each other. I don't want or need your apologies or anything from you. I just want you to leave me alone. Let me raise my baby and take care of her."

"I get that," he says. "But I'm not the same guy you met back then. I'm sober and healthy now, and I can't just let you walk away with *our* daughter while I turn a blind eye and pretend she doesn't exist. I get why you didn't tell me. I was beyond fucked up back then, in no place to father a child, and you did what my mother never did… You protected our daughter." He reaches out and slides his knuckles down my cheek. "But I'm here now, and I want a chance to get to know her, to be the father she deserves."

I step back out of his touch. "No."

"No?"

"No," I repeat. "I won't do this again. I won't put her in harm's way. I've been there, done that, got the graves to prove it, and I won't risk her life. I learned the hard way that when I'm up against drugs, I lose every damn time. It's too late for my son, but I can still protect Aurora."

"I'm sober," he says again. "I go to meetings several times a week. I haven't touched a drug in fourteen months, I swear. I just want a chance..."

I bark out a humorless laugh. "You don't think I've heard all this before? I was married to the King of Chances. Gave him chance after freaking chance. No! No, no, no! I'm all out of chances."

I grab the handle of the stroller and am about to walk away when Gage grips my bicep gently but strong enough to prevent me from leaving. "I know this is hard for you, but I can't let you walk away. That little girl is mine too."

"What are you trying to say?" I ask, twirling around and removing myself from his grip.

"I'm saying that I want to be in her life, and I'm asking that you give me a chance to be her dad, please. I don't want to take this to court..."

"Fuck you! I don't care who you are. I don't care that you're some famous drummer for some popular band or that you're worth millions of dollars. My job is to protect her!"

"And I love that you want to do that," he says, keeping his calm. "All I'm asking is to be given the chance to get to know her. Please, Sadie. I don't want to fight, and I'm not trying to take her away from you. I just want to see my daughter."

I stare at Gage as his eyes bore into mine, begging, pleading, and my heart drops into my belly, knowing that I'm going to have to give in. I might be able to keep him away temporarily, but if he goes to court and proves he's sober, they'll give him rights to her because he is her father. And what if he tells them I kept her away, and they try to punish me? The thought of my little girl being taken from me has the blood in my veins turning cold.

"Fine. You can see her."

Gage sags in relief. "Thank you. When?"

"Today, I guess. Since we leave tomorrow."

His brows furrow. "Sadie, I don't just mean once. I want a

relationship with her."

"I get that, but we live in Virginia, so unless you're moving there, it will have to be done over the phone. We have an entire life there. A home… I have a boyfriend." More like a guy I'm kind of, barely dating, but I don't mention that.

"I… I can't just move to Virginia," he says, dragging his fingers through his hair. "The band is recording…"

"If making music is more important than seeing your daughter, then that's your problem." I know I sound like a bitch, but I'm not the one with the drug problem who fucked me and then fucked those other women while he was high. He's the one who pushed me away. He's the reason I moved to Virginia. And I'm not about to make this easy on him. I made shit easy on Vincent and look where it got me. Never again.

"No, it's not," he finally says, sounding defeated. "I'll figure something out. Where are you staying?"

"At the W."

"The one near Bryant Park?"

"Yeah."

"That's near me," he says. "If you want, we can go there and order in dinner. Then once Aurora wakes up, we can spend some time with her. There's a park nearby that Kendall and Layla take the kids to."

"Who?" I ask, confused.

"Layla and Kendall… They're the wives of Declan and Camden, my friends and bandmates. I think you met Declan, right?"

"Yeah, and Braxton and Kaylee as well."

"They're good people." He smiles softly. "Anyway, the studio is near Bryant Park, so they take them to the park there a lot."

"Okay. Yeah, we can do that."

We walk through the cemetery in silence, and when we get to

the end of the sidewalk, a man rounds the front of the SUV and opens the back door.

"I have a stroller," I say to Gage.

"It can go in the back."

"Her car seat is at the hotel."

"Oh, shit… I mean, shoot. Umm…" He looks around like he's hoping a car seat will suddenly appear out of thin air.

"Just meet us there," I tell him. "I need to change and feed her anyway, and when she wakes up, she's cranky, so she'll need a few minutes."

"That's okay. I can walk with you guys."

The guy standing there clears his throat.

"This is Paul. He's part of our security team."

I nod toward the tall, muscular man, who's the same height as Gage—and with the muscles Gage has added since the last time I saw him, pretty much the same size as well—confused.

"He keeps the paparazzi in line," Gage notes. "We generally don't walk anywhere or take the trains because it can get crazy when a fan recognizes us. It happens here less frequently than in LA, but with me showing my face again and the band announcing that we're back in the studio, it's been a little hectic lately."

"Okay… Well, I'm not going to run with our daughter, so just meet me at the hotel. I'm staying in room 252."

And with that, I walk away, stroller in hand, wishing I never came back here, praying Gage really is sober, and hoping he doesn't destroy my entire world.

Thirteen

Gage

I HAVE A DAUGHTER. A BLUE-EYED, RED-HAIRED, FAIR-SKINNED, BEAUTIFUL LITTLE GIRL. She looks like the spitting image of her mother, except she has my eyes and curly hair. I don't know anything else about her, though. Her likes, dislikes, when her birthday is… Nothing. But that's going to change. I never imagined having kids, especially not after…

Fuck, I just can't believe it. When Kaylee sent me the image, I knew deep down she was mine. But I was hoping I was wrong. Because if she was right, that would mean while I was getting high, overdosing, and spending months in rehab, Sadie was growing a baby we created in her, giving birth, and raising our daughter alone.

Because I fucked up. I pushed away the first woman I'd connected with in years. I got scared and did the unforgivable. I fucked two women in my living room, knowing Sadie would see. Knowing it would hurt her, and she would walk away from me. I couldn't even tell you what either of them looked like or what their names were. I remember nothing but the look on Sadie's face when she walked out and saw what was taking place. The hurt in her eyes has haunted me for months. It's the reason I didn't look her up or go after her once I was sober. Because she deserves better than what I did to her.

God, it now feels like forever ago, another lifetime, but that's how life works. I might be sober now, but the effects… the consequences of my shitty choices will continue to darken my door. Although is it really a consequence when the result is that beautiful baby girl?

And Sadie…Goddamn, she looks good… *gorgeous.* She was on the skinny side when I found her at the cemetery because she wasn't eating properly. She was beautiful but sad—eyes glassy and features etched with devastation. Now, she looks happy. Her eyes were clear and bright. Every time she'd look at our daughter, she got this twinkle in her eye. She was meant to be a mom.

And a wife. When she told me she was in a relationship, I wanted to punch something. Of course, she's with someone. I barely know her, and even I know she's the whole damn package. The thought of some other guy spending time with my daughter makes me feel sick. Him stepping in and playing daddy… Do they live together? Does my daughter think he's her dad? Are there family photos of them hanging on the walls? After they put Aurora to bed, does he take Sadie to their room and get lost in her?

When we were together sexually, it wasn't about attraction with her. It was about the escape and losing ourselves in one another. I was too high to fully appreciate her body or treat her the way she deserved. But now… she's got curves for days. If I were given another chance, I would take my time and worship every damn inch of her.

I shake those thoughts from my head. She's with someone now. I lost my chance. I chose drugs over her, and that's my punishment: to have to look at her every day, knowing we created a beautiful little girl and we'll never be a family. At least it's not too late for me to be a part of Aurora's life. I don't blame Sadie for keeping her from me. She did what she felt was best, given the situation and her past, but shit has changed. I'm sober and have every intention of being a father to my daughter. I grew up without a dad, and I'll be damned if my daughter does the same.

Kaylee: Is she yours?

I add Kendall, Layla, Braxton, Camden, and Declan to the chat so I don't have to repeat myself.

Me: Sadie's daughter is mine. Her name is Aurora... She calls her Rory, and they've been living in Virginia. She's leaving tomorrow to go back. I'm going over there now to spend some time with them.

Kaylee: I can't believe she kept her from you!

I never told anyone what happened that night, the last night I saw Sadie, but now I have to because I can't have my friends hating the mother of my daughter.

Me: I deserved it. Sadie lost her son and husband when he drove while high and got into a car accident. I found her mourning their deaths (along with the baby girl she miscarried the day before their accident). I brought her to my apartment and spent months with her. When Braxton told us he was moving in with you, Declan asked if Sadie and I were getting serious. I got scared and brought two women home. While I was high on heroin and coke and pills and whatever the fuck else I had taken that night, I fucked them in the living room. Sadie saw and walked away. She had to save herself, and I'll never blame her for that. When she found out she was pregnant, she made the decision not to tell me about Aurora because she was doing what a mother should do...protecting our daughter from me. Do

not hate her for that. I don't. Now, I have to prove to her that I'm capable of being a father to our daughter.

A few minutes go by before the texts flood in…

Kaylee: I'm sorry. I didn't know. ((hugs))

Declan: You're not the same person you were back then.

Braxton: We're here for you…

Camden: You're going to be a good dad.

Layla: I respect what she did. I would've done the same thing.

Kendall: If you need anything, please let us know.

Me: Thank you. I'll let you know how it goes. Just got here.

Paul pulls around back so I can take the private entrance up to Sadie's floor. Once we're at the door, I tell him I'll give him a call when I'm ready to go. When Sadie opens the door, the sleeping baby is now awake, attached to her hip, her blue eyes, identical to mine, looking at me curiously.

"Thank you for letting me come over."

Sadie nods. "I'm sorry for being so… mean earlier. I—"

"You don't owe me anything, least of all an apology," I say, cutting her off. "You're hurt and scared, and I deserved everything you said. The fact is, we barely know each other, but we share a daughter, and I'd like to get to know you both. I know I have a lot to prove, but I'm hoping you'll give me the chance."

She sits on the couch with Aurora, who drops her head onto her mom's shoulder and eyes me shyly yet curiously while I sit in the chair across from them.

"I can't believe we have a daughter," I muse, unable to take my eyes off her. "Can you tell me about her? What's her middle name?

When's her birthday?" There's so much I want to know, and I feel like I don't have enough time. It's already almost dinnertime, and they leave in the morning.

"Her middle name is Rebekah… Aurora Rebekah Sharp, but as I mentioned before, I usually call her Rory for short."

When she says her name, Aurora pops her head up, giving her mom an adorable toothy little smile. "Mama." She presses her tiny hands to either side of Sadie's face and places a loud, wet kiss on her nose, making Sadie laugh and my heart jump straight the fuck out of my chest.

"Aw, you give me kisses?" Sadie asks, her voice soft and filled with love. It makes me wonder if my mom ever spoke to me like that. The only memories I have are of her crying. She was always sad and down, never could get ahead. When I was old enough to understand how rough shit was, I can remember thinking that one day I would make enough money that she would finally be able to smile. Never got the chance, though.

Aurora answers Sadie's question by giving her another kiss before she scrambles down and plops onto the ground, crawling over to a bin of toys.

"She'll be one on May fourth," Sadie says, her eyes following Aurora as she dumps a bunch of toys out and grabs one, bringing it straight to her mouth. When she seems entertained, Sadie turns her attention back to me. "Rebekah was—"

"Your baby girl," I finish, recalling the name of the baby she lost. It's on the gravestone, and even though I was high all the damn time back then, I remember her telling me about her.

"Yeah," she says softly. "I wanted to honor her since she never had the chance to be part of this world."

"It's beautiful and perfect. And you gave her my last name?"

Pink tints her cheeks. "I did… I wanted so badly to tell you about her, but I was just so scared. When I saw on the news that you overdosed and almost died." She swallows audibly. "I just couldn't do it," she breathes, tears filling her eyes. "I kept imagining what happened to Collin, happening to her, and…"

"Stop," I tell her, crossing over to the couch and pulling her into my arms. "I hate that I missed out on the first ten months of her life and that you went through your pregnancy and giving birth without me, but you did the right thing. I'm clean now, but it was a long-ass road to get here. I'd like to think had I known about her, I would've gotten clean quicker, but there's no way of knowing."

Sadie looks up at me, and I thumb away the straggling tears resting on her cheeks. "I was so lonely and tired," she admits, breaking my heart. "So many times, like when Rory was in the NICU, and I was scared, or when I brought her home, and she was up all night crying, and I wasn't sure what was wrong, I wanted to reach out and tell you just so I wouldn't be so alone, but the fear of what could happen if you showed up high was too strong."

"I'm so fucking sorry," I rasp, hating myself for putting her in that position, for not being the guy she needed and could count on back then. I've failed so many damn people in my life but letting Sadie and our daughter down hits the deepest because she's already been hurt and let down, and when she needed someone the most, I not only pushed her away but inadvertently pushed my daughter away as well.

"She came eight weeks early and spent two weeks in the NICU while her lungs finished developing," she says, once she's gotten ahold of herself. Backing up slightly, she pulls her phone out of her back pocket and scrolls for a few seconds before turning it around so I can see what's on the screen.

"That's her?" I ask, taking in the tiny little human with wires all over her, lying in a rectangular glass container.

"Yep. Four pounds, one ounce." She flips to the next picture of her holding Aurora. The woman in the photo is filled with exhaustion, black circles under her eyes, but there's also a soft smile of happiness there. The next several photos are of Aurora getting older: smiling, laughing, crying. Sitting up, crawling... It's insane how in only ten months, she's transformed from an itty-bitty little thing to a crawling, babbling, laughing baby.

"She's put on some weight," I say with a laugh when she flips to a picture of Aurora in the bathtub, bubbles covering her lower half and the top half filled with adorable baby rolls. Kendall and Declan's babies have them too. Declan always jokes, saying they eat too much even though they're both breastfeeding.

"Did you breastfeed?" I ask. It doesn't matter either way, but I want to know everything. I hate that I won't know unless I ask, but I did this to myself.

"I did. She actually recently weaned off, and her pediatrician said since she's so close to a year old and healthy, she can go straight to milk and regular food. She loves sweet potatoes and carrots and hates anything green." She laughs, putting her phone away as Aurora crawls over with a cup of some sort in her mouth.

She pulls herself up and hands it to Sadie. "Mamamama."

"She also loves stacking things and knocking them over," Sadie says, taking the cup from her daughter and then picking her up. She walks over to where Aurora just was and plops down, setting her in her lap.

I watch as Aurora helps Sadie stack the cups, one on top of each other. When they place the last one, Sadie cheers and claps, and Aurora joins in, just before swinging her fist and knocking them all to the ground. For a second, she stares at them, then she looks up at me and giggles. Fucking giggles. And my heart—my bleeding, battered, blackened heart—comes back to life.

As I'm frozen in place, Aurora grabs a cup, bites down on it, and crawls over to me, stopping just before me and dropping it into my lap.

"She's sharing with you," Sadie says softly, snapping me out of it.

"Thank you," I say awkwardly. Aside from chilling with Felix, Layla and Camden's six-year-old, I don't have much experience with kids, especially not with babies. I'm around Declan and Kendall's twins, but I haven't interacted with them much. They're around six months old and just now trying to crawl. They do this weird rocking back and forth thing that makes them look like little turtles trying to take off. It's kind of hilarious.

"Baba!" Aurora yells when I don't move.

"She wants you to build the tower," Sadie explains, a hint of a smile on her face.

"Oh, all right. Sure." I take the cups from Sadie and start to build the cup tower while Aurora watches with a glint in her eye, silently conveying she's about to cause destruction. The second I set the last cup on the top, she claps, not stopping until I join in.

I watch as she makes sure I'm clapping and excited before she swipes her hand out and sends the tower to the ground, cups flying every which way. Her eyes meet mine, and she giggles that fucking giggle, and once again, my heart feels as though it's been resuscitated.

"Baba!" she squeals, grabbing a cup.

"She could do it a million times," Sadie says, playfully rolling her eyes when I take the cups and start stacking them again. "You don't have—"

"I've missed out on ten months," I say, not allowing her to finish her thought. "If she wants me to build this tower a hundred times, I'm okay with that." Our eyes connect, and Sadie nods in understanding.

And that's how we spend the evening: building towers and

knocking them over until Aurora is hungry and starts to whine. Sadie feeds her some baby food while I order us dinner. And once it arrives, Aurora eats some more. She reminds me of an adorable little bird as she opens her mouth, and Sadie feeds her little bits of her food. As I watch the two of them sitting across from me, for the first time in years, my heart feels so damn full. Wanting to take a few photos of my daughter, I pull my phone out and snap a few pictures of them eating and laughing.

When Sadie sees what I'm doing, she turns Aurora around and says, "Say cheese." Aurora obviously doesn't say that, but she does giggle, which is even better. I take another picture, then switch it to video so I can capture the sound, knowing when I'm back home and alone, and they're over seven hundred miles away, it'll be the only thing I'll have of my daughter to get me through until the next time I can see her.

Fourteen

Gage

WHEN IT'S TIME FOR HER BATH, SINCE SADIE DOESN'T KICK ME OUT, I STAY AND WATCH, memorizing every babble, every giggle, dreading the moment when they leave to go back to Virginia.

Sadie lets me participate in Aurora's bedtime routine by reading her favorite book to her and explains that she usually goes to sleep earlier at home, but being here has thrown her off a little bit. Not being at home in her room has messed up their structured routine.

"Can I come visit?" I ask once Aurora is fast asleep in her portable crib.

"Gage…" Sadie sighs, shaking her head. "I… I don't…"

"I know," I say, not needing her to finish. "This is all a lot to take in. I get that, and I know you have a boyfriend, but fuck…" I glance at the sleeping beauty who's half mine. "I want a chance to get to know her."

Sadie's eyes fill with liquid as she nods. "Can we please just take this slow? She doesn't know you, and it's just all so unexpected."

"Yeah, of course," I say, willing to agree to anything that will get me time with my daughter. And then a thought hits me. "Does your boyfriend…?" I clear the emotion from my throat. "Does Aurora think he's her dad?" I choke out.

Sadie's eyes go wide. "No." She shakes her head to emphasize her answer. "No, he's never even met her."

I sigh in relief.

"We only recently started dating, and I didn't want to bring her around him unless we were serious. My best friend from college, Sarah, lives in Virginia, which is why I moved there. She's married with two kids, busy running her own spa. When I first moved there, I didn't know I was pregnant, but it worked out. Rory is close to the same age as her youngest, so sometimes, she'll watch her so I can have some alone time." She shrugs. "Between working full time and Rory, it's easy to forget to make time for myself."

Speaking of which… "How are you on money?"

She narrows her eyes, and I quickly raise my hands, waving the metaphorical white flag. "Sadie… It's obvious you take care of our daughter just fine, but the last time I saw you, you were homeless."

She sighs and nods in understanding. "I wasn't homeless. I just didn't want to go home. It was the last place I saw my family alive, and it was too hard. After you…" She clears her throat, ready to skip over what I did, but one of the most important parts of recovery is facing what I've done, so before she can continue, I finish the sentence for her.

"After I brought two women home and had sex with them in the living room."

Her eyes fill with hurt. "Yeah," she whispers.

"Sadie…"

"Gage, I don't really want to go there. We weren't together, and you didn't owe me anything."

"Maybe not, but what I did was still wrong. There were a million other ways I could've pushed you away, but I chose the one that would hurt you the most."

"Why would you want to hurt me?" she asks, her voice small.

This isn't exactly the way I want to end my time with her, but it's a conversation that needs to be had... One she deserves.

"The reason I had a drug problem was because my high school girlfriend committed suicide... and I'm the one who found her."

Her eyes go soft, and she moves closer to me. "I'm so sorry."

"She had been lashing out for a while, but she wouldn't talk to me. After she died, I found a note from her that said her stepdad had been raping her for months. He was threatening to send her away and hurt me. She had tried to tell her mom, but she wouldn't listen. It all became too much, and she felt the only way out was to end her life."

"That's horrible."

"It was. My mom was murdered when I was twelve in a motel room where she was prostituting. They claimed it was an accidental overdose, but I'd seen her pimp shoot her up too many times. When Tori died, I felt like I failed her and my mom, so to cope, I started using.

"The band took off for LA, and we quickly hit it big. The next several years were a whirlwind of recording and touring. The guys tried to get me help several times, but I wasn't ready. I was a functioning addict."

She nods in understanding but doesn't say anything, letting me explain.

"When I met you, I was teetering on the edge. While we were together, I toned it down a bit, getting lost in you. It had been so long since I connected with another person that I craved you more than the drugs... just barely.

"The night you found me with those women, Braxton announced

he was officially moving out and in with Kaylee, and Declan asked if you and I were getting serious and if I planned to move you in or get our own place.

"Realizing how close we'd gotten scared the shit out of me. I had already failed my mom and Tori, and you had lost so much. I knew I wasn't in a place to take care of you like you deserved, so I went out and got fucked up, then brought those women back, knowing once you saw them, it would push you away."

Her pouty lips curve into a small frown, and I hate myself all over again for what I did. "I was using heavy shit, Sadie. Heroin and coke... I don't even remember that night, to be honest. But when I woke up and found your letter, enough surfaced for me to put the pieces together. The day you walked away began my downward spiral, ending with me hitting rock bottom."

"The overdose," she whispers.

"Yeah. It all just became too much. I was missing you and hating myself for what I did to you. I went to the cemetery and visited Tori... and I just..." I shake my head, the words failing me.

"Did you mean to overdose?"

"Yeah, I did," I admit. "It was a moment of weakness, but that's all it takes. Declan found me, and they saved my life. I checked into rehab and spent the next ten months getting sober."

Her brows shoot up. "Ten months?"

"Ninety days in rehab, then seven months in isolation with my sponsor and therapist. I needed time to figure my shit out. I'd spent so long being high, I wasn't sure how the hell to function sober and clean."

I pull my keys out and show her my most recent chip. "It's glow in the dark." I shrug. "One year clean." I flip to the other one I keep on my keys. "One day at a time."

"I'm so proud of you, Gage," she says, placing her hand on mine that's holding the tags.

"Thank you." I sniff and place the keys back in my pocket. "A part of recovery is going to meetings and seeing a therapist, but another part of it is facing the shit I did while I was high, which includes facing what I did to you. I know it's going to take time for you to trust me, but I'm going to work every day to earn it. To show you I'm not that guy."

"I hope so," she says, her voice wobbly. "Vincent swore so many times he was clean, and I know you aren't him, but you have to understand that drugs are a hard limit for me, so trusting you is going to be extra hard."

"And I'll just have to work extra hard to earn your trust," I tell her. "Now, you were saying… After I hurt you and you left, you went home?"

"Yeah. I went home and finally mourned. I cried and cried until all the tears dried up. Then I cleaned out the house and put it up for sale, only keeping some of Collin's things, like pictures he drew and photos I took… I gave Vincent's parents his stuff since I didn't want any of it.

"The day I learned who you were from the news running the story of you overdosing, I also learned I was pregnant. I was already living in Virginia and renting a two-bedroom home, living off the little bit I made from the sale of the house. Between that and the savings we had put away, I could afford to be home with Rory. But I love working, so recently, I started working again. I'm an editor, so I can work from home. I do it when Rory is napping and after she goes to bed. It keeps me busy and stops my brain from turning to mush."

"You're amazing," I tell her, meaning that wholeheartedly. She was at her lowest, lost her entire world, and managed to turn her life around all on her own.

"I don't know about that," she says shakily.

"You are." I take her hands in mine. "Thank you… for being the mother and father Rory needed. I promise you, from today forward, I'll be there in any way I can be. I know you don't need the money, but I'm going to pay you for back child support." She opens her mouth to argue, but I don't let her speak. "Please. She's my daughter too, and I want to take care of her. It's bad enough I won't be able to see her every day. Please let me at least do this."

She swallows thickly and nods. "Okay. And to answer your earlier question, yes, you can come visit. Just… please don't make me regret it."

Fifteen

Gage

"OH, MY GOD, SHE'S SO FREAKING ADORABLE," KAYLEE SAYS, WATCHING THE VIDEO OF Aurora giggling. "And her eyes are totally yours. And her nose… well, aside from the nose ring."

"When can we meet her?" Layla asks, watching the video over Kaylee's shoulder.

"I'm not sure," I admit. "They're back in Virginia, and Sadie asked that we take things slow." It's been three days since I've seen them in person, but every night before bed, Sadie has called me so I could say good night to Aurora.

"Makes sense after everything she's been through," Declan says.

"I'm having back child support sent over to her, and she agreed to send pictures every day. I was thinking maybe this weekend I'll fly there and see where they're living and spend some time with them." I haven't spoken to Sadie about it yet, but when she calls tonight—if she calls—I'm going to bring it up.

"I'm very proud of you," Sophia says, squeezing my shoulder. "You're handling this all very well. If you need anything, you know we're here for you."

"I know, and I appreciate it."

The truth is, I'm not handling this well at all. I've been to two NA meetings and had an emergency session with my therapist. Finding out that I have a daughter who I missed ten months with because of my addiction has been rough. I have a lot of regrets, and I can't help feeling like I've already failed her and Sadie.

I started seeing Viola—my therapist here in New York—once I moved back when Pamela recommended I have someone to talk to in person. She understood where I was coming from but also pointed out that I can't change the past, which is something I have issues with.

With my mom, I wanted to go back and save her. Same with Tori. Now, I regret not getting my shit together sooner, so Sadie wouldn't have had to go at it alone, and Rory would know I was her dad from the beginning. But I can't change any of that. All I can do is make shit right moving forward, which seems damn near impossible when they live over seven hundred miles away.

"All right, ladies, lunch has been fun, but we need to get back to work," Camden says, standing and giving Layla and Marianna a kiss.

We spend the next few hours hammering out another song and nailing down the instrumentals with our producer. The songs are coming along smoothly, and if we continue like this, we should be able to start officially recording in the next few weeks.

As we're finishing up for the day, my phone vibrates in my pocket, indicating an incoming call. Sadie's name flashes across the screen, so I click accept, and her face, along with Rory's, displays.

"Hey Gage, are you busy?" Sadie asks.

"Nah, we're just finishing up in the studio." I stand and wave to the guys, giving Sadie my full attention. Braxton follows me since we rode together because I'm still staying with him and Kaylee.

"If you want to call back—"

"I'm good." There's no way in hell I'm going to turn her away when she calls me. I don't care where I am or what I'm doing.

"Okay, well, it's Rory's bedtime." Every night she's called me around this time, so I can "be there" to say good night to Rory.

"Did you guys have a good day?" I ask, walking through the hall and out to the awaiting SUV. Braxton doesn't say a word, but I can tell he's listening as he sits beside me.

"We did. I finished editing a book, and we went to the park. Rory's new favorite thing is the slide, and I swear she went down it a hundred times. Oh! And another tooth came through. She now has four teeth." She smiles, looking so proud, and I feel so damn lucky that my daughter has such an amazing mom.

I connect my AirPods and stay on the phone while Sadie reads Rory a bedtime story and then goes through kissing her good night. And then she points the phone in my direction and says, "Rory, wave bye-bye to Daddy," and holy shit, my heart implodes in my chest at the word Daddy. It's the first time she's referred to me as Daddy, and it's officially my favorite word.

Rory smiles lazily at the screen and lifts her hand, her fingers squeezing open and closed, and I do the same to her. "Good night, Rory," I say. "I… I love you and miss you," I choke out, needing her to know. She's too young to know the words or understand what I'm saying, but that won't stop me from saying them.

Sadie swallows thickly. "Night, Gage."

"Night. Thank you for calling."

We hang up, and I sit in silence, staring at my phone, wishing I could be there with them. Seeing my daughter for five minutes a night isn't enough, but I don't know what else to do. I pull my keys out of my pocket and glance at the tag I got when I started NA: *One day at a time.* I need to remember this.

"Hey, man, I'm going to go to a meeting," I tell Braxton when we pull up to his place and get out.

"All right." He pats me on the shoulder. "I know we've all said it, but we're here for you. You've been thrown a major curveball, and it's got to be a lot to handle."

"I did this to myself. If I wouldn't have been high…" I take a deep breath, remembering what Viola said about the past. "Rory's not a curveball. She's my daughter. I just need to figure out how all the pieces fit. I hate them being so far away."

"I didn't mean it like that. I just meant that you were heading in one direction, and suddenly, you're being spun in circles. It's okay if you don't figure it all out right away. You only just found out about her a few days ago."

"Because I was an addict and fucked up big time. Rory and Sadie deserve better than this shit."

"Speaking of which…" Braxton smirks. "From what Declan said, you and Sadie were pretty hot and heavy before. Any chance you two have picked up where you left off?" He waggles his brows, and I groan.

"Are you two seriously gossiping like a couple of chicks?" I punch him playfully in the arm. "Quit it."

"Still didn't answer the question."

"Her husband was an addict. He's the reason her son is dead. I met her crying on their graves, unable to go home after she lost her entire fucking world." I glance at the bustling pedestrians and cars on the road. "She didn't tell me that I have a daughter out of fear of history repeating itself. The only thing I can hope for is a chance to be a father to Rory.

"Besides, she's already seeing someone. She said it's not serious, but…" I shrug.

"What if she was willing to give you a chance?"

I think back to the way she felt in my arms, in my bed. The way we could talk for hours or just simply walk in silence. Even as fucked up as I was back then, I knew Sadie was a fucking keeper. It's why I pushed her away. And that was when she was at her lowest, grieving and devastated. Spending time with her now... Fuck, I already know she's the whole damn package. She's got a good head on her shoulders, is a damn good mom to our daughter, is sweet and forgiving—I mean, even hurt and pissed, she still let me in—and gorgeous... beyond gorgeous.

"I'd scoop her up so quick and never let her go," I admit. "I'd spend every day of our lives making sure she never hurt again. Making sure she felt loved and cared for. She spent so many years caring for others, putting up with her husband's shit, my shit. When she walked away, she wrote me a note..." I swallow thickly, remembering the words. I've looked at them every day since she walked away. "Even after I hurt her, she still told me she believed in me. Told me to fight and find happiness."

I choke up, wishing I could go back and make better choices. "She could've been my chance at happiness, but I fucked it all up," I admit to Braxton. "Now, my punishment is that I'll have to watch someone else be her happiness."

"I think you should talk to your therapist," he says, shocking the hell out of me since we rarely discuss my recovery. "You *both* deserve happiness, and there's no reason you can't be each other's. Yeah, you messed up, but you don't deserve to be punished for it."

After going to an NA meeting and chatting with Gabe for a while, I text Viola, asking for an emergency session. She's available an hour later, and we spend our time talking about the possibility of Sadie and me.

"What would you think about me meeting her?" Viola asks at the end of our conversation.

"Rory?"

"Well, her too. But I meant Sadie. As the mother of your daughter and the woman you clearly have feelings for, I would love to speak to her to see where she stands. Even if you two don't end up together, you'll be co-parenting for the rest of your lives. Maybe the next time you talk, you can bring it up and see what she thinks. It's up to you."

The next few days fly by, filled with music and Sadie and Rory from afar. I'm missing them like crazy, so when the guys mention taking the weekend off to spend time with their families, I ask Sadie if I can come visit, telling her I'll stay in a hotel so it's not awkward. Thankfully, she agrees, and Saturday morning, I'm on an early flight out. Since the town she lives in is quiet, I leave Paul behind and rent an SUV at the airport.

On the way to Sadie's place, I stop and pick up breakfast and coffee, remembering what she liked from our time together.

She opens the door with Rory on her hip, and as I stare at the two of them, dressed in their pajamas with their messy hair, Rory's head resting on Sadie's shoulder, my heart feels as though it's whole again, and I know whatever it takes, I need to make both of these girls mine.

"WHAT THE HELL IS THIS?" SADIE HISSES, WAVING HER PHONE IN THE AIR, WITH HER FACE red in anger. We've spent the day together. After Sadie let me spend some time with Rory while she showered and took a little bit of time for herself—I offered after she mentioned Rory was up all night and she was exhausted—we took Rory to the park, stopped for lunch at Sadie's favorite deli, and then ordered in dinner. We did the whole bedtime routine together, and I read Rory her story before she fell asleep. The day has been perfect, and I can't wait to do it all over again tomorrow.

Not wanting to overstay my welcome, I helped Sadie clean up, then went to kiss Rory good night one last time before heading out, but when I walked out to say goodbye to Sadie, I found her at the table fuming.

"I'm not sure," I tell her, walking over.

"This," she says, punctuating the word as she shoves the phone into my face.

It takes me a second to see what I'm looking at, but once I do, I frown in confusion. "That's your child support paperwork. I told you I was going to pay back child support. My attorney insisted you sign the paperwork as proof that you understand you're receiving it." I shrug. When I told him about Rory and Sadie, he told me he would take care of it. He wanted to file for joint custody, but I didn't want to jump ahead and put Sadie on the defense. My hope is we'll figure it all out together, but I figured while we're doing that, I could show her I'm serious by paying her what I owe her. It's at least a start...

"Yeah, I can see that. There are way too many zeros. Are you trying to pay me off or something?" She glares my way. "If you think you're going to pay me off and take my daughter from me—"

"Whoa," I say, shaking my head. "Have you heard of Raging Chaos? I make a damn good living. Even taking the last year and a half off, I still have income coming in, and my financial advisor knows his shit, knows how to properly invest, so while I wasn't doing shit, my money was still multiplying. I would never try to take our daughter from you... ever."

"Shit, I'm sorry. I was just in shock. But Gage, that's a lot of money. Like the kind of money people ask for when they kidnap a kid and want ransom."

I chuckle at how adorable she is. "It's seventeen percent of what I earned during the ten months Aurora has been alive. That's what child support is based on in New York."

I can tell when she does the math in her head because her eyes go wide. "Holy shit."

"Aurora is my daughter too," I tell her, sitting at the table across from her. "Which means it's my job... my *right* to take care of her as well."

"You're right," she finally says. "Thank you."

We're both quiet for a few moments, and my thoughts go back to my conversation with Braxton the other day. I glance over at the television and take a chance. I know she has a boyfriend, but it's not like I'm propositioning her for sex. "It's still early. Want to watch a movie or something?"

Her eyes widen before she averts her gaze. "I should probably get some work done," she says, standing. "Rain check?"

"Yeah, sure." I nod and stand as well, taking the hint. "See you tomorrow?"

"Yep. See you—" She flinches. "Shit, tomorrow..."

"Yeah... Sunday."

"I know." She rolls her eyes. "Sarah was actually supposed to take Rory for the afternoon. Mark had asked me to go to a show with him."

"Who?" I ask, even though I have a feeling I already know.

"Mark. He's the guy I'm... dating. I can cancel..."

"I can stay with Rory," I blurt out.

"While I go on my date?" she asks incredulously.

"You aren't going far, right? I watched her while you showered. I played with her and changed her diaper and got her dressed. It will give me a chance to spend some more time with her, just the two of us, and she seems comfortable with me. I know her routine…"

"I don't know," she says, looking a mixture of confused and sick.

"I won't go anywhere with her," I promise, knowing that's a hard limit for her after what happened with her late husband and son. "If there's an emergency, I'll call for help."

Her eyes bug out. "Gage, this is a lot. A big responsibility. I'm sorry. It's just too much, too soon. I can't… not yet."

My heart drops, but I don't argue because I get it. It's one thing to be with Rory while Sadie is in the other room. It's a whole other thing for her to leave Rory with me alone. It's going to take time for her to trust me, and I need to be patient.

"I don't want to fuck with your plans," I say instead. "I can come over in the morning and play with Rory while you get ready, and then take off once you're ready to go."

"You sure?" she asks slowly.

"Yeah, I'm sure."

She walks me to the door, and even though I probably shouldn't, I lean in and kiss her cheek, my lips lingering for a fraction too long on purpose. "Thank you for today. I had a really good time."

"Of course," she squeaks out, telling me she's not entirely unaffected by me. "I'll see you tomorrow."

I spend the rest of the night writing music, the words flowing. I don't know if it's being sober or spending time with Sadie and Rory, but lately, I can't stop putting my thoughts and feelings onto paper. When I send them to the guys, asking what they think, Camden says he wants to add it to the album, and the other guys agree.

Braxton: Does this mean you crashed and burned?

I roll my eyes at his question. The truth is, I was expecting it. I can't write a song about a guy wanting a woman who wants someone else without it raising questions.

Declan: With Sadie? Wait, is this song about her? She has

a boyfriend??

Me: Yes, she has a boyfriend, and no, I didn't crash and burn.

I wouldn't call asking her to watch a movie and getting turned down crashing and burning. That was me just trying to put feelers out to see if she would even be willing to spend some time with me alone—which she wasn't.

Me: Sadie's the mother of my daughter and nothing more. Leave it alone.

Thankfully, the guys listen, and the texts stop for the night, but that doesn't stop me from thinking about her and how much I wish she could be more.

Sixteen

Sadie

"OH, SWEETIE." I PUSH THE SWEAT-COVERED HAIR STRANDS OFF RORY'S FACE, HATING that she's not feeling well. There's nothing worse for a parent than having to watch your child go through being sick and feeling helpless.

The day after Sarah watched her, while I went on my date with Mark, she called and said her kids were both running fevers and had all the symptoms of a cold. She apologized, not knowing they were coming down with something, and I told her she was being ridiculous. We can't possibly know every time our child is going to be sick. She could pick up anything from anyone: at the park, at a restaurant… germs are part of life.

That night, Rory woke up from a coughing fit in the middle of the night. The next morning, the sniffles came, and along with them came the fever. Now she's tugging on her ear in pain, and I'm sure it's due to an ear infection.

"I'm going to call the doctor right now," I tell her, pressing a kiss to her warm forehead. While I'm making the appointment, she falls into a coughing fit, getting so worked up that it ends with her throwing up.

"Mamama," she cries, fresh tears filling her lids.

"It's okay, sweet girl," I tell her, my heart cracking in two. "We're going to give you a bath and then take you to the doctor."

The pediatrician confirms she has an ear infection, then mentions it sounds like there's wheezing in her chest, and that she's concerned about her being dehydrated, which leads to hours at the hospital while she's given chest X-rays and hooked up to an IV with fluids.

Thankfully, her lungs are clear, but after her labwork comes back, the doctors diagnose her with RSV, and since she was born premature and RSV can be severe, they insist on keeping her overnight to monitor her. Since the safest place she can be is at the hospital, I don't protest it, but have you ever had to force an eleven-month-old to sleep at a hospital?

By the time she's discharged with a nebulizer and prescriptions for her ear infection and cough, I'm so beyond exhausted. When we get home, I prop the mattress of her crib up with a pillow underneath in the hopes of her getting some sleep, and I crash in my own bed.

My eyes are barely closed when there's a knock on the door. I jump up, praying to the sleeping gods that it doesn't wake Rory, and run to answer it. When I open the door, I find Gage looking a mixture of scared and pissed off.

"Are you guys okay?"

"What?"

"I've been calling you for the past two days, and you haven't answered!" he barks. "When you didn't call me two nights in a row for bedtime, I got scared and got on a plane."

Oh, shit! "I'm so sorry," I whisper, opening the door so he can come inside. "Rory got sick, and I gave her my phone to watch a show in bed, and it must've died. I took her to the doctor, and we ended up staying in the hospital overnight, and I was just so worried and exhausted, I forgot about my phone."

Gage's features morph from pissed to worried. "Rory's sick? Is she okay? Why the hell didn't you call me?"

"I…" I begin, ready to make an excuse but cut myself off because no matter which way I slice it, I'm in the wrong. "I forgot," I admit, shaking my head. "I'm so used to doing this all myself that I literally forgot about you. I'm so sorry."

Gage's face falls, and I feel like the biggest piece of shit. He's been trying so hard to be in our daughter's life, even though he's long distance. I would be so mad if I found out she was sick and in the hospital, and Gage forgot to tell me.

"Can I see her?" he asks, his voice resigned and distant.

"She's sleeping, but you can go peek in."

He nods and walks to her room. A few minutes later, he comes back out. "Can I come back tomorrow and see her?"

"Of course," I say, stepping toward him. "Gage, I really am sorry. I was just scared, and it was all a lot. She has a respiratory virus, which can be serious for babies born prematurely, and an ear infection. I went into mom mode and blanked out. It doesn't by any means make it okay, but I just want you to know I didn't not tell you to exclude you. You're her dad, and in the future, I'll make sure to keep you informed."

"It's okay," he says softly. "I appreciate it. Is she okay now?" Somehow, him not yelling or getting mad makes me feel worse. If the situation were reversed, I would've freaked the hell out on him.

"She's on medication for her ear infection and cough and has to do the nebulizer twice a day. I also have a vaporizer going in her room."

He nods. "That's good. Do you need anything?"

"No. I'm just tired. It's been a long couple of days."

Another nod. "All right, well, I'll get out of your hair and let you get some sleep. I need to go see if the hotel has availability. I'll be back in the morning."

"Or you can stay," I blurt out.

He quirks a brow.

"I have a guest room. Well, it's my office, but there's a bed in there. That way, you don't have to spend money on a room." Another pop of his brow. "You'll be here in the morning when Rory wakes up." This gets his attention.

"You sure you're okay with that?"

"Yeah, of course. You're her father. I really am sorry for not calling you."

"All right," he says. "I'll stay. It'll be nice getting to see her in the morning when she wakes up." He smiles softly. "Thanks."

After showing him the bedroom and then saying good night, I head to bed, knowing all too well Rory will be up bright and early, and if I don't get some sleep, it's going to be another long-ass day.

MY THROAT ACHES WHEN I SWALLOW.

My eyes burn.

An itch in the back of my throat bubbles up and forces me to cough.

Dammit, I'm sick.

I knew this was a possibility, but I was hoping the vitamin C I've been popping would help my immune system. Guess not.

I groan, reaching over to take a sip of my bottled water, and then wince when it hurts going down. Just great. Nothing more fun than trying to care for my sick baby while being sick myself.

And then it hits me: sick baby. Why isn't my sick baby crying? What time is it?

The sun peeking through the blinds tells me it's daylight.

I jump out of bed and run down the hall, finding Rory's room empty. And then I remember Gage spent the night. My heart picks up speed. He wouldn't have taken her anywhere, right?

He was upset that I forgot to tell him that she was sick, but he wouldn't have just up and left with her to punish me.

Oh, God! What if he left to get breakfast with her?

Memories from the past surface.

Me miscarrying.

Sleeping in.

Vincent taking Collin to get breakfast.

Neither of them ever coming home.

"Oh, God, please no."

"Hey, you okay?"

I twirl around and find Gage standing in the doorway with Rory attached to his hip.

"Oh, thank God. I thought…" I shake my head, unable to finish my thought.

"You thought I left with Rory," he finishes, his lips curving into a frown.

"Yeah," I breathe.

"I told you I wouldn't," he says. "She woke up a little bit ago, and you were coughing like crazy, so I didn't want to wake you up. I changed her diaper and fed her breakfast, and we've been watching some good ole *Sesame Street* on the couch."

"They still make that show?"

"I don't know, but I found it on YouTube, and she seems into it."

"Thank you," I tell him. "I'm sorry for—"

"Stop apologizing. This is all new to both of us. It's going to take some time, but we'll get there… one day at a time." He smiles softly. "Why don't you help me give Little Miss Sick her meds and then take some yourself and go lie back down? I can chill with her while you get some rest."

I sigh in relief, thankful to have Gage here with us, especially now that I'm sick as well. Going through her meds, I give her the cough and ear medicine before popping some meds myself and then going back to bed.

I pass out instantly, not waking up until it's dark outside. Confused and disoriented, I check the time and see it's eight o'clock. Holy shit, I literally slept all day. I go pee and brush my teeth, then walk out to check on Gage and Rory, finding them in her bathroom. I stand in the doorway, watching as he gives her a bath. She must be feeling better because she's splashing away and laughing as he pretends one of her toys is a shark coming after her to tickle her.

As I watch them together, a feeling of warmth spreads through my chest. I don't regret my decision to walk away and later protect her, but I'm glad that, unlike Vincent, Gage has committed to getting and staying clean. I wonder if I would've pushed harder and forced Vincent to go to rehab if things would've been different, but then I remember what Gage had said one night when we were talking about his recovery—that nobody can force an addict to get help. He has to want to do it himself. And Gage wants to be clean.

"Hey, how're you feeling?" Gage asks, shaking me from my thoughts.

"My throat hurts, and I have a cough, but not too bad."

"Good. I got you some chicken noodle soup." I stiffen at his words, and he must notice because he adds, "I had food delivered."

Dammit, I did it again. I assumed the worst without giving him the benefit of the doubt. It's not fair to continue to project my insecurities and past on him when he's trying so hard to move forward. He's been clean for over a year and deserves to be given the benefit of the doubt.

"Thank you. Soup sounds really good."

"Mamama!" Rory yells, her hands coming down and splashing her and Gage.

"Hey, sweet girl." I walk into the bathroom and lean down to kiss her forehead. Did you have a good day with Daddy?" She answers by splashing again, this time giggling.

"Go eat, and once she's done, I'll put her pajamas on and bring her out to say good night before I put her to bed."

"Thank you," I choke out. "You being here... means a lot to me." Too many times, Vincent would choose the pills over being a husband and a father. I spent years wishing and hoping for a partner, only to be alone. Gage doesn't understand what him being here really means to me.

Gage deserves a fresh start, to be given the chance to be the father he's trying to be, and it's time to give him that chance.

Seventeen

Gage

"AND THEN THE PINK PRINCESS WITH HER PINK TUTU DANCED ACROSS THE STAGE. THE end."

"Dada," Rory squeals, slapping the book closed and climbing off the couch. I swear every time she yells *Dada,* I want to give her the damn world. Setting the book down, I follow her as she crawls across the floor to her favorite cups. She's dressed in a pink onesie and tutu that matches the book I just read to her, and she looks so damn cute. I snap a picture of her and send it in a group text to my friends, and seconds later, the women are texting back that they can't wait to meet her.

Sadie is still under the weather, so she's been sleeping a lot the past few days, leaving me to spend time with Rory. As she hands me the cup, silently demanding I stack them with her, I have no clue how the hell I'm going to walk out the door tomorrow and get on that flight to go home. Every day I spend here makes it harder to leave. A month ago, I didn't even know I had a daughter, and now I can't imagine living without her... except I don't actually live with her. I visit... occasionally. Since I've known about her, I've spent more days on the phone with her than in person... until this week. And spending time with her, watching as she grows and changes, makes me realize everything I'm missing when I'm gone. And it fucking sucks. But what choice do I have?

As I stack the cups, Rory falls into a coughing fit, and I check the time to see if I can give her some more medicine. She hates taking it, throwing a tantrum every time, but eventually, she gives in, and it helps.

"Time for medicine," I announce, lifting her into my arms and carrying her to the kitchen. The second she sees the medicine, her eyes fill with tears, and I wish I could snap my fingers and make her and Sadie better. Unfortunately, life doesn't work that way, so I set her on the counter, holding her so she doesn't fall, and fill the syringe with her cough medicine. She whimpers, her bottom lip jutting out, and my heart breaks.

"I know, princess, but it's going to make you all better," I tell her.

"Hey, is she okay?" Sadie asks, stepping into the kitchen. Her eyes are a bit puffy, and her hair's a damn mess, but fuck, if she isn't as beautiful as always. Every time I look at her, I'm reminded of what I had and lost.

"Yeah, I just gave her some cough medicine." I carry Rory back into the living room and set her down in front of the cups. She immediately remembers that she never knocked them down and swipes her hand out, sending them crashing to the floor with a laugh.

"It's the little things," I joke, making Sadie chuckle.

Rory grabs a cup and stands, glancing at her mom, sitting in the loveseat several feet away.

"Mama!" Rory babbles, trying to hand her the cup.

"Come here," Sadie says, extending her arms. Up until now,

Rory's refused to walk unless she's moving across the furniture, so when she takes a step toward Sadie, Sadie's eyes go wide in shock as I whip out my phone.

"Mama!" Rory yells as she puts one foot in front of the other. I get every step on camera, not stopping the recording until Rory's in Sadie's arms and she's giving her daughter kisses, telling her how proud she is of her.

"Let's see if she does it again," Sadie says. "Ror, give Daddy the cup." Rory's eyes go straight to me, and the fact that she knows who I am has me choking up with emotion.

Sadie sets Rory on her feet, and instead of her dropping to her knees, she starts walking toward me, waving the cup in the air while she smiles wide. "Dada!"

I watch her, frozen in place, as she wobbles over to me. Once she arrives, I lift her into my arms and kiss the tip of her nose. "Look at you walking."

"I can't believe she's walking," Sadie says, smiling at Rory.

"I got it on video. I'll text it to you."

"Thank you. She seriously needs to stop growing. It's like every day she wakes up, she's speaking more words, doing something new… growing out of her clothes." She sniffles. "Sometimes, I feel like I took being a mom for granted with Collin. I was so busy dealing with Vincent that I didn't get to enjoy Collin like I do Rory. It's probably not healthy, but I want to spend every minute with her, not wanting to miss a single moment."

"It's not unhealthy," I choke out, feeling the same damn way. "You know what it's like to lose people you love, so it makes you appreciate those in your life that much more."

159

"HEY, WHAT'S GOING ON WITH YOU?" CAMDEN ASKS, WITH ONLY CONCERN LACED IN HIS words. It's been five days since I left Sadie and Rory to come home. I didn't want to leave, especially not with both of them still somewhat sick, but I couldn't leave the guys hanging, and we had the studio scheduled to nail down more songs. We're almost halfway done with the songs, and then the recording will begin. When I told Sadie I needed to go, she didn't argue. Just simply thanked me for being there and said she'd see me soon. She might not need me, but fuck, if I'm not starting to need them.

They call me every night, but it's not enough. Not after spending five days with them. Waking up with them, having breakfast with them. Getting to see my daughter every day. Watch her walk for the first time… By the time I was reluctantly saying goodbye, she was crying for me and not wanting me to leave, and fuck if that didn't make it that much harder to walk away.

The problem is, I can't be in two places at once.

"Gage? What the hell, man? You've missed the cue three times now. You need a break?"

"I'm sorry," I say, snapping out of it. "I'm good."

Camden stares at me for a long beat, then nods. "All right. Let's take it from the top."

He starts to count down when my pocket vibrates with an incoming text. I yank it out in case it's Sadie, and sure enough, it is.

Sadie: Rory's cough has taken a turn for the worse. She's having trouble catching her breath, and they're admitting her to the pediatric unit at the hospital to monitor her. I'm here now, but there's no service, so I won't be able to talk. I'll call you when I can.

I've barely finished reading her text when I'm jumping out of my seat and heading for the door.

"Gage!" Camden barks. "Where are you going?"

Shit! I forgot where I am. "Rory's having trouble breathing. She's been admitted to the hospital. I gotta go," I choke out, hating that in order to be there for my daughter, I'm letting the guys down, but my daughter will always come first. "I'm sorry…"

"What? Don't apologize," Declan says. "Go be with your daughter. Let us know if you need anything."

I nod and haul ass out the door. On the way to the airport, while I'm looking for a flight, Easton texts that the Blackwood jet is available, and he's already let them know to get it fueled and ready. I thank him and then text Sadie to let her know I'm on my way on the chance it will go through.

A couple of hours later, I arrive at the hospital. A nurse shows me to Rory's room, and when I walk in, the sight in front of me damn near sends me to my knees. Rory is in the crib with Sadie sitting in a chair next to her. Both girls are asleep—Rory wheezing softly while Sadie's head is pressed up to the bars of the crib, her hand outstretched through a bar and her fingers laced with our daughter's. I imagine Rory scared and crying and Sadie trying to comfort her, and my heart cracks open, blood dripping all over the damn floor.

I should've been here. Sadie shouldn't have to go through this on her own. She's not the only parent, and she deserves to have a partner by her side. My mom never had anyone, and I won't let that happen to Sadie. I can't have my daughter growing up and thinking it's the norm to see her dad more over the phone than in person. And it's not fair to the guys for me to keep taking off and leaving them hanging. It's also not good for me to keep stretching myself thin. I want… *no, I need* to stay healthy and clean, and I can't do that if I'm constantly being tugged in every direction. If I feel like I'm failing everyone, including myself.

As I watch Sadie and Rory sleep, I consider every option, every road in front of me to take, and even though it's going to hurt like a bitch, I know what I have to do.

I step outside and consider if I should call or text the guys. It's late, and they're probably with their wives and kids, so I choose to text them—I'm also a fucking pussy and, even though it needs to be done, I hate that I have to do it.

> **Me: You guys will never know what it means to me that you had my back all these years, that you waited for me and refused to move forward until I was ready, but I can't be part of the band anymore. My entire world is in Virginia, and I can't be in two places at once. Any songs I wrote or contributed to, I'll sign over to you guys. I'm sorry, but you need to look for a new drummer.**

I hover over the send button, and once I hit it, bile rises up my throat, and I run to the bathroom, throwing up everything in my stomach. Then I turn my phone off so I can focus on my daughter and walk back inside her room, refusing to regret my decision.

A little while later, Sadie wakes up. When she sees I'm here, she looks a bit shocked to see me, like she wasn't expecting me to fly out to be with her and our daughter, and I promise myself she'll never have a reason to doubt me again.

"How's she doing?" I whisper, handing her a bottled water I grabbed from the shop.

After she downs half the bottle, she says, "Okay, I guess. They have her on a mechanical ventilator to help get good oxygen in and the bad out. They explained it all to me, but it's a lot to process. She was so mad and fought them, so they sedated her to calm her down." Tears fill her eyes, and I cut across the room to pull her into my arms. "I was so scared, Gage. One minute, she was fine, and the next, she was having trouble catching her breath. I thought…" She sniffles. "I thought she was going to die."

"Nothing's going to happen to her," I vow even though I have no right to say that. "You did the right thing bringing her here." I situate us on the couch with her in my lap, and surprisingly, she lets me. "You're an amazing mom, and our daughter is so fucking blessed to have you."

She snuggles into my chest and sighs. "Thank you for coming."

"You don't ever have to thank me for being here for our daughter. This is where I belong… and I won't be leaving anymore."

Her head pops up in confusion. "What?"

"I told the guys I'm leaving the band. I can't keep being in two places at once, and where I belong is with Rory…and you."

"Gage…"

"I know you have a boyfriend, but you're the mother of my daughter, and we're going to be spending the rest of our lives raising her together. Just please let me in as her father. That's all I'm asking."

She nods in understanding. "For the record," she murmurs, putting her head back down to my chest. "I no longer have a boyfriend." I still at her words. "He wasn't happy about being kept on the outside, and I couldn't let him in. So I ended things."

"Can you let me in, Sadie?" I ask, tipping her chin up to look at me. "I know it's scary as hell, especially with how shit started with us, but can you give me a chance, please?"

"I'm going to try," she says. "You're right. It is scary, but I'm really going to try."

The next several days are filled with doctors and nurses and a very upset Rory, but thankfully, the ventilator does what it needs to do, and with her medication, she's released with a clean bill of health. Since I came without any clothes, and I refused to leave my daughter, the nurses were nice enough to bring me scrubs I could wear and offer us a shower to use.

Rory is still groggy from all the medications, so when we get back to Sadie's place—which I paid to be completely cleaned and sanitized—she plops onto the couch next to me and rests her tiny head against my arm.

"I'm going to go shower," Sadie says, smiling over at us as I turn on the television and click on one of Rory's favorite shows.

"Take your time. We're good."

I pull my phone out that I've been neglecting and scroll through the messages from the guys, asking me to think about this before I make any rash decisions. It's easy for them to say that when their entire world is under one roof, but in order for me to be with my daughter, I have to drive eight hours or get on a plane.

Since I came with nothing, I'll have to go back and pack, and then I need to find a place to live here near the girls. It's going to take a little bit, but at least once it's done, I'll be near them.

Me: I'll be back soon to get my stuff, and I can sign whatever paperwork you need me to sign.

Declan: I really wish you would reconsider. We can figure shit out.

Me: It's not fair to you guys or to Sadie and Rory for me to always have one foot out the door.

Camden: We get it.

Braxton: Yeah, but we sure as hell don't like it.

Eighteen

Sadie

"ALL RIGHT, SWEET GIRL. WHAT DO YOU SAY WE GO TO THE PARK AND GET SOME FRESH air?" Rory shrieks and wobbles toward the door at the mention of the word park. "First, we have to get dressed." I laugh, lifting her into my arms and carrying her to her room.

We're both finally free of illness, so it will be nice to get out. It feels like we've been cooped up in the house—or hospital—for weeks. I've just finished changing her diaper and getting her dressed when there's a knock on the door. Gage didn't mention returning today. Actually, aside from saying he's moving here once he gets everything sorted, he didn't specify when that would actually be taking place.

"Let's go see who it is," I tell Rory as I walk to the door. I check the peephole and recognize the woman. At first, I can't remember from where, but then it hits me.

"Hello," I say when I open the door. "How can I help you?"

Kaylee, Braxton's wife and Gage's good friend, smiles softly at me. "I'm Kaylee Lutz," she says, extending her hand.

"I know, Braxton's wife. We met when I was staying with Gage a while back."

She nods. "May I come in? I was hoping we could talk."

"Sure." Rory's shyness toward strangers has her clinging to me when I try to set her down. "Would you like something to drink?" I ask, remembering my manners. "I have coffee, water, juice…" I cringe, and Kaylee laughs.

"I'm good, but thank you." She smiles at Rory, who peeks at her through her lashes, curiously. "She's beautiful. With your red hair and Gage's blue eyes, Gage will be scaring the boys off left and right when she's older."

"Oh, God," I groan jokingly. "She just started walking. Don't turn her into a teenager yet. I don't think I can mentally handle that."

Kaylee laughs. "I met Gage when we were in high school. He was best friends with Declan, Camden, and Braxton, and I was best friends with Tori and Layla." At the mention of Tori's name, I go still.

"The guys' dream was to make music. Every day, we hung out in the studio while they wrote and played. Everyone knew they were going to blow up. They were that damn good. The music seeped from their pores. They lived and breathed it like it was an extension of them. I can't remember a day when Gage didn't have those damn drumsticks sticking out of his back pocket." She laughs, but it sounds far away as if she's reliving that time in their life. I stay quiet, letting her say what she obviously came here to say.

"Gage never had a real family growing up. He had his mom, but she wasn't all there, and he spent more time as a kid trying to take care of her than she took care of him. The day he met Camden, though, he found his family. The moment Camden welcomed him into the fold, the guys became inseparable. Where one went, they all followed. I didn't become close with them until our sophomore year, but everyone knew those boys were more like brothers than friends.

"When his foster parents all but kicked him out when he turned eighteen, Cam's parents even insisted he live with them. And when Tori died, they helped him move forward the best they could."

She sniffles back emotion. "The guys knew he was struggling with drugs, but he wouldn't talk about it. When I went on tour with them, I saw it for myself and told them they needed to do something, but they were too close to Gage. They loved him and accepted him the way he was. They knew he was still grieving, and instead of pushing him to get help, they enabled him."

I nod in understanding, knowing all too well how that works. One of my biggest regrets is not forcing Vincent to get help or, at the very least, walking away from him when I knew he wasn't going to get the help he needed. It's easy to point fingers at the family and friends, but I know firsthand that it's not that easy to force someone to get help.

"For a minute, he started to calm down a little. He didn't seem to be using as much…"

"When we were hanging out," I say.

She nods. "We all hoped you'd be the one to save him, but we had no idea that you weren't in any place to save yourself, let alone him." She smiles sadly, and I know Gage told them about my past.

"After you left, things got bad, and he tried to end his life." She swipes at a tear, then glances down at Rory, who's now sitting on the couch flipping through the book that she can't read.

"I'm not in any way blaming you, especially now knowing what he did to make you leave. I just wanted to give you the whole story…"

I nod and sigh, thankful Gage didn't make me out to be the bad guy. "It really hurt," I choke out. "I know that we weren't together, and promises weren't made, but it still really hurt."

"What he did was wrong on so many levels, and I'm sure it makes it really hard to trust him again."

"I can tell he's changed," I admit, needing to give him some credit. A few times while he was here, I heard him talking to his therapist, and more than once, he said he needed to go to a meeting. "But yeah, it's still hard to let him in, but I'm trying."

Kaylee smiles softly for a few seconds before her features morph into a frown. "When he left for rehab, we thought it would be ninety days, and he'd come home clean. But ninety days turned into ten months. The guys refused to play without him. They wouldn't record a single song until he came home because they're more than a band... They're family.

"It took Kendall and me going to him to bring him home because he was scared of how things would be now that he's sober. He didn't want to fail anyone or let anyone down. He views Tori's and his mom's deaths as his failures. And now, ever since he found out that he's a dad and you've been doing it on your own, he thinks he's failed you and Rory." I don't miss that she calls her Rory instead of Aurora—a nickname only I, and now Gage, call her. Which means he's been telling them about her enough that she knows her nickname.

My stomach drops, and now I understand where she's going with this. Gage is moving here, giving up the band to be with his daughter, to make sure he doesn't fail us, which means he's leaving the only family he's ever known and ultimately failing them.

"I didn't ask him to move here," I blurt out, suddenly feeling like I need to be on the defense.

"Oh, I know," she says gently. "It was his decision. He's torn between being in New York with the band and being here with you and Rory. But he doesn't want to be away from you guys anymore."

She leans forward and locks eyes with mine. "Gage doesn't know I'm here, and he probably would be pissed if he knew I was, but I had to come and plead with you. Beg you not to make him choose."

I swallow thickly with where this is going. "This is my home. You can't expect me to move back to New York for Gage. He might be doing good right now, but he's still an addict. What happens when he starts using again?" I say, shaking my head. Moving to Virginia was my fresh start. I hate that I'm not near my son's and daughter's graves, but in a way, it's for the best. It forced me to move forward, to focus on myself, on healing. If I go back...

"His entire family is there," Kaylee says. "His therapist and sponsor and his meetings. He needs us," she chokes out, "and we need him. The guys need him. I know it's selfish of me to ask, but please, don't let him walk away from us, from the band. It took him so long to get here, to be sober and finally start living again. If you would just be willing to move there, he could have everyone and everything he loves in one place. He needs this, Sadie. He needs to record this album sober and know that he did it, that he didn't let his brothers down. Please, give him that.

"I know you don't owe him that, and he might not even deserve it, but please. He needs it."

Tears prick my eyes, hearing the emotion in every word she speaks, but I don't think I can do it. I don't think I can move there and leave my home and the little bit of support I have behind.

"I'm sorry," I whisper. "I just... I don't think I can do it."

Her face falls, but she nods in understanding. "It's okay. I had to try." She stands and smiles sadly. "If it's okay, could we come and visit one day? Like an actual official visit? Gage has sent us so many pictures and videos, and he doesn't stop talking about you two. Everyone is dying to meet you both."

"Of course," I say, standing to walk her out.

Once she's gone, I spend the day with Rory, but I can't stop thinking about everything Kaylee said. When bedtime rolls around, like every night, we FaceTime Gage. He's usually at the studio or in his room, but tonight when he answers, it looks like he's around a bunch of people.

"I'm sorry, you're busy…"

"What? No," he says. "I'm at the Blackwoods." He moves his phone so I can see everyone. "This is Easton and Sophia, Camden's parents."

I don't know how I didn't put it together until now, but I immediately recognize Easton as the pop star that I spent many years listening to… still do. "Hey," I say, suddenly shy.

"This is Sadie and my princess Rory."

Rory hears her dad's voice and instantly perks up. "Dadadada!"

Gage beams. "Hey, princess," he says softly.

"Hey, Sadie," Sophia says, her smile filled with kindness. "We've heard so much about you. Hopefully, we can meet you one day."

"That would be great," I say.

"Oh, Gage," a woman says, forcing her way into the picture. "She's so beautiful. Look at that red hair. They're both beautiful."

"This is Layla," Gage says, rolling his eyes playfully. "Camden's wife."

"Hi!" She waves.

"I wanna see da baby," a little girl says, crawling onto Gage's lap.

"This is Cam and Layla's daughter, Marianna. See the baby?" he says to her. She nods. "That's my daughter."

"Baby!" Marianna says at the same time Rory says, "Dadadada!" grabbing the phone and pulling it to her face as if she can touch him through it if she gets close enough. Her lips press against the screen, and she makes a kissing sound.

"She's giving you kisses," I say with a laugh, pulling the phone back.

Gage smiles sadly. "I'll be there soon," he says to Rory. "Then you can give me real kisses."

My heart drops as everyone around him goes quiet, obviously knowing what him coming here means—leaving them.

"We can call back in a little bit," I say through the lump of emotion that's filled my throat, making it hard to breathe.

"Nah, just give me a second to go somewhere quiet. Sophia makes the best food, so when she demands I come over for dinner, I can't say no."

I nod, unable to say anything. I know he's not doing this on purpose. He doesn't know Kaylee was here earlier, but I'm questioning everything now after hearing her and seeing all of the family and support Gage has in New York.

Once he's alone, I read Rory her book, and then we both say good night to Gage. After I give her two kisses—one from me and another from Gage—I leave the room, closing the door behind me.

"I've been looking at places," Gage says once I'm back in the living room. "I'd like to see them in person before I sign a lease, so I'm going to stay at the hotel for a little bit until I decide which place is my best option. I was, umm…" He clears his throat. "I was wondering if maybe, after a while, I could take Rory to my place. Maybe once you can trust me enough, she can spend the night. You could spend the night too…" My eyes go wide, and he backpedals. "I mean, like, so you know she's safe with me. Not like that. Although, if you wanted…" He scrubs his hands over his face. "Fuck, this is all coming out wrong."

I snort out a laugh. "It's okay, I get it. We'll figure it out. One day at a time, right?"

"Yeah," he says softly. "One day at a time."

"OH, GOD, THIS IS SO CRAZY," I SAY FOR THE MILLIONTH TIME AS I PUSH A SLEEPING RORY down the street in her stroller. "What was I thinking? What if this is a mistake? A huge mistake?" I mutter to myself as I walk into the Blackwood studio where Gage texted me a little while ago, saying he was. Apparently, he's there to sign a bunch of papers to terminate his contract. So instead of meeting him at the hotel, I came straight here to stop him.

After I got off the phone with Gage, I sat in the living room thinking about everything and weighing my options. I came to the decision to move back to New York so he wouldn't have to leave his band, and he would get to see Rory every day. Before I could second-guess my decision, I packed us a bag and booked us a flight. And now, here we are, walking up to the front desk at Blackwood.

"Hello, how may I help you?" the woman asks.

"I need to see Gage Sharp."

She snorts a laugh. "I'm sorry, ma'am, but this is a closed studio. If you—"

"Sadie?" a masculine voice says. I glance over and find Easton, dressed in a suit, walking over. "What are you doing here? Is everything okay?"

"Yes... No." I sigh. "Gage said he was here."

"He is. Is he expecting you? We're about to go into a meeting."

"That's why I'm here," I say, then take a deep breath, knowing if I say the rest, I can't take it back. It wouldn't be fair to Gage to say I'm moving here and then change my mind. "I've decided to move here... so Gage doesn't have to leave the band."

Easton's eyes widen, and then a smile splits across his face. "Oh, Sadie." He pulls me into a hug. "Thank you, but are you sure?"

"I am. I need to talk to him first, but yeah, I am." I've spent the entire night and morning thinking this through.

"All right, then how about we go see him, yeah?"

I follow Easton down the hall and into the large room where Gage and the rest of the band are all already sitting.

"Sadie," Gage says, noticing me immediately. "What's going on? Is everything okay?"

"I need to talk to you…alone."

His brow furrows, but he nods. "Okay…" He glances around. "Can we use your office?" he asks Easton.

"Yeah."

Gage walks us down the hall and into a gigantic, over-the-top office filled with records and expensive wood and plush furniture. I'm so distracted by it all that I forget what we're doing until Gage says, "Talk to me."

"I want a contract," I blurt out. "I want it in writing. If you do any drugs, whether it's powder or pills or even smoke weed, you forfeit your rights to Rory." Gage's eyes bug out, and I groan, hating the way that came out. "I'm moving here… Rory and I are moving here, so you can stay and play," I explain. "I'm an editor and can do that anywhere, but you need to be here with the band. And you have family here. I don't… I don't have anyone. Not really."

"You have me," he says, stepping toward me. "If you let me in, you have me."

"I'm scared," I admit, trying like hell to push back the tears. "That's why I want it in writing. I want you to be tested every few months, and if you come back positive for any kind of drugs, you have to let Rory and me walk away. I know that seems harsh, but—"

"No, that's not harsh," he says. "Your late husband lied to you, and you need the reassurance. I understand, and I agree."

"You do?"

"Yeah, I'll sign whatever you want because I *know* I'm never using another drug again." He glances down at Rory and then back up at me. "I have too much to live for."

I sigh in relief. "Thank you for understanding."

"No." He shakes his head. "Thank you. You have no idea what this means to me… you being here." He envelops me in a hug. "I'm going to earn your trust, Sadie, one day at a time. And then…" He pulls back and looks into my eyes. "I'm going to earn your heart."

Nineteen

Gage

"GAGE... WHAT DO YOU MEAN, MY HEART?" SADIE ASKS, LOOKING A MIXTURE OF SHOCKED and nervous. I didn't mean for it to come out the way it did, but now that it's out there, I might as well own my intentions.

"I want you," I tell her straight up. "I messed up back then and wasn't in a place to start something with you, but I knew, even blitzed out of my mind, that you were a keeper. And that's what I want... to keep you."

She swallows thickly, and I cup the back of her neck and look into her beautiful emerald eyes that remind me of a fresh start. "I know it's going to take time for you to let me in, but I need you to know my endgame. It's you and me and Rory under one roof. And not because we share a daughter.

"I felt it back then, the connection we shared, in *and* out of bed, but I was too damn scared and high not to fuck it all up. I pushed you away, thinking it was for the best, wanting you to move forward and find love and happiness, but there were so many days I considered reaching out, especially once I was clean, wanting to beg you to give me another chance. And then I find out you had my baby.

"Fuck, it's like fate stepping in on my behalf. And I would be a damn fool not to take advantage of this second chance I've been given."

She sighs into my touch. "I get it. Even back then, I felt the connection between us while I was grieving, but I don't know if I can put myself out there again. I'd like to think I've healed from my past, but the pain goes beneath the scars, where nobody but me can see."

"I get it," I tell her, feeling her words in the deepest part of my soul. "I think that's what drew me to you. Our shared pain. Knowing no matter what we do, we'll never be the same again."

She nods in understanding. "I want to try, to see where things go. I can't make any promises, but I want to try."

"That's all I'm asking. For a chance." I frame her face and press my lips softly against hers, breathing in her scent for several seconds before I back up and give her some space.

"I should probably get going," she says softly.

"Where are you staying?" I ask, still in shock that they're really here. One minute, I was sitting down to sign the paperwork to terminate my contract with Blackwood, and then the next, I'm kissing her in Easton's office after she tells me she's moving here… for me.

She shrugs sheepishly. "I didn't exactly think this through."

"Sadie." I cup the side of her face. "Are you sure about this? If you need to think—"

"No, I'm sure. I just didn't think through how it would all unfold." She laughs nervously. "I rented a room at the W temporarily. One day at a time, right?"

"We'll get it all sorted," I promise. There's no way I'm going to let her and our daughter sleep at a hotel long term, but this came so out of the blue, I'm going to need a minute to gather my bearings and get everything figured out.

"Dada," Rory says, her voice gruff from sleep.

"Yeah, princess, I'm here." I kneel in front of her stroller, watching as she rubs the sleep from her eyes.

"Dada." She sits up and lifts her arms, wanting me to take her out. "Dada!"

"We really should get out of here." Sadie laughs. "I imagine you have band stuff to do, and the last thing anyone wants is this crazy child being let loose."

I chuckle at how adorable she is. One thing about Blackwood Records is that it's family-oriented. Someone's kid is always hanging around. "Or you could stay," I tell her. "The guys will be stoked to find out that I'm still in because of you. I'd love to introduce you to them in person."

"You sure they won't mind me crashing?"

I pick Rory up, and she hooks her little legs around my hip, her arms wrapping around my neck. "Nah, they're going to be excited to meet you."

Sadie pushes the stroller behind me as I guide her back to the office where I left the guys waiting. When we enter, they stand, all looking a mixture of nervous and curious.

"Sadie's moving here," I announce. "I'm not going anywhere."

The guys whoop and cheer while Declan picks up Sadie and swings her around. "You are the damn MVP," he says, setting her down. "Thank you."

"Hell yeah," Braxton says, picking her up next. "Thank you."

"This means so much to us," Camden says once she's back on her feet. "Seriously, we can't thank you enough. We were just plotting how to somehow convince you to move here."

"His wife already did," Sadie says with a light laugh, glancing over at Braxton.

"What?" I ask. "Kaylee spoke to you?"

Braxton groans. "I should've known. Let me guess, yesterday?" Sadie nods. "When she disappeared for several hours, I knew she was up to something. She didn't threaten you, did she?" Braxton grimaces, making Sadie laugh.

"No, she was very sweet. We spoke, and she gave me a lot to think about. I'm an editor and can do that from anywhere, and the truth is, New York is my home. Not particularly the city, but I love it. I ran from it, but it's time I came home."

I make a mental note that Sadie doesn't like the city. My goal is to find her—well, hopefully us—the perfect house, and knowing that she prefers the suburbs helps.

"This calls for a celebration," Camden says. "I say we take the day off and head over to my place for a barbecue, get to know the newest members of Raging Chaos." Camden tickles Rory's side, and she giggles, snuggling closer to me.

"That sounds perfect. What do you say?" I ask Sadie. "Up for it?"

"Sounds good."

"OKAY, SO HEAR ME OUT," KENDALL SAYS, WIPING HER MOUTH.

We've just finished eating delicious burgers Declan grilled, along with a bunch of sides the women whipped up when the guys told them we were coming over to celebrate the band moving forward. Ever since we arrived, the women have been all over Sadie and Rory, wanting to get to know them. I've never been so thankful to have the friends that I have. When Sadie mentioned she needed to get going soon to check in to her hotel so she could get situated, everyone looked at her like she was crazy.

"I have a condo near the studio." Kendall looks from me to Sadie. "It has two bedrooms, two baths with an upstairs loft that can double as a playroom, and a gorgeous view overlooking Bryant Park. I was renting it out since it's not really a seller's market right now, but the tenant had to break his lease to move for work. With a good cleaning, it will be move-in ready."

"Wow," Sadie breathes. "That sounds amazing. I'd like to eventually find a place outside of the city, but for now, that sounds perfect. How much would it be a month?"

Kendall's eyes flit over to me, and I shake my head, silently telling her it's not happening. There's no way in hell Sadie is paying shit, especially when she came here for me. "I'm sure we can figure something out," she says. "If you want, I can show it to you tomorrow."

"That would be great. Thank you."

We hang out for a little longer, the kids all playing while the adults bullshit, and when Rory gets cranky, making it clear it's time for her afternoon nap, we say bye to everyone, so I can take them to the hotel. The guys and I will be back in the studio first thing tomorrow, but I want the rest of the day with my girls to get them situated. I hate that I don't have my own place to bring them back to, but I'll be doing that while I work on winning over Sadie.

"She went out like a light," Sadie says with a laugh, plopping onto the seat next to me.

"She played hard."

"Yeah, she did." She smiles softly. "I loved watching her play with everyone. Aside from Sarah and her two kids, it's usually just Rory and me. I've been thinking about joining some kind of mom's group, but they're a bit intimidating," she says with a laugh. "Your friends, on the other hand, are so warm and welcoming."

"They like you," I tell her, turning to face her. "And they're not just my friends. They're my family, and they can be yours too, if you want them to be."

She smiles. "I think I'm going to take Kendall up on her offer. I have no clue about the city in terms of where to live, and if she lived there, I'm sure it's nice."

That's an understatement... Kendall's place probably costs a month what most pay a year for their mortgage, but I don't mention that, not wanting her to change her mind. Kendall is a huge pop star and wouldn't live anywhere that isn't top-notch. I've never been there, but I have no doubt it will have the best security and top-of-the-line everything. It will be the perfect place for Sadie and Rory to live while I figure everything out.

Speaking of which... "There's something we should talk about."

She quirks a brow. "Okay."

"As you know, I'm part of Raging Chaos, and while New York is a hell of a lot tamer than LA, with us recording again and announcing our next album and single soon, plus doing some promo shit that goes along with releasing, people, especially fans and the paparazzi, will come out of the woodwork. With me being gone, they want answers, to figure out where I've been and what I've been up to. I'd like to post about you and Rory to beat them at their own game, confirming I have a daughter before they can fly in like vultures and attack.

"That also means, though, that you're going to need a guard with you and Rory when you leave." Her eyes go wide, so I explain before she jumps to the wrong conclusions. "Nobody's going to hurt either of you but having someone with you means if they get too close, take shit too far, you'll have someone to protect you. They're nosy fuckers and will want to get your pictures and ask questions. Rory's and your safety are my top priority. If we were living in LA, it'd be insane, but luckily, New Yorkers are chill for the most part. I just don't want you to be blindsided by it all."

I edge closer and cup the side of her neck. "I know it feels like a lot, but shit will calm down, I promise. Aside from the months when we're releasing and touring, our lives are pretty normal."

She snorts out a laugh. "Yeah, okay. That's cute that you're trying to keep me calm, but I've seen the videos and posts and know nothing about your life is normal... but it's okay, I get it. I'm not going to run... unless you push me away again, that is."

"That's never happening," I vow. I take a deep breath, then ask her something I've been wanting to ask but have been afraid to. "How would you feel about meeting Viola, my therapist? She mentioned you attending a session with me, not only because of us possibly dating but also because we're co-parenting Rory. I just..." I swallow thickly, trying to word shit correctly. "I want to make sure you know how serious I am about staying clean, that you feel like you can talk to me about anything."

I hold my breath in fear that it's too much too soon, and I'm going to scare her off. My fear deepens when tears prick her eyes until she speaks. "I don't want to compare you to Vincent because it's not fair to you, and I'm working on not doing that, but so many times I asked him to speak to someone, and he would tell me he was, but when I would ask if I could join him, he'd tell me he wasn't ready. I learned that he wasn't really seeing anyone, that he would lie and work late instead, so you inviting me to meet with your therapist means the world to me, and I would love to meet Viola and speak with her. I want to support you in any way I can. And not just as the woman who you're *possibly* dating..." She smiles a watery smile. "But as the mother of your daughter, who you're co-parenting with, and… as your friend."

After we hang out and talk for a bit, I make my exit, not wanting to overstay my welcome. But not before I ask if she'll come by the studio tomorrow. She's never seen me work, and I know Rory is too young to really understand it, but I'd love for her to see me in my element, to have them there as part of my world. She says she'd love to come by, so we plan to go see the condo afterward.

When I walk in the door, I find Kaylee and Braxton sitting on the couch. He's holding her while she cries in his arms.

"What's wrong?" I ask. I was with them at the barbeque earlier and they seemed fine.

"Oh, nothing," Kaylee says, waving me off.

"It's not nothing," Braxton adds. "We've been trying to get pregnant, and we thought she was. The test showed positive."

"But I'm not," she says through her tears. "Apparently, you can have a missed miscarriage. It happens to a lot of women, and they don't even know it."

"I'm sorry," I say, hating that two of the best people I know are struggling to get pregnant, when they'll make amazing parents. Sometimes, life is just plain fucked up.

"Thanks." Kaylee releases a deep sigh. "So, Sadie seems really sweet…"

"Yeah, she is. Thanks for what you did… going to see her."

Kaylee's cheeks stain pink. "I didn't want to overstep, but I was afraid she didn't know how important music is to you."

"It's not as important as her and Rory, but I'm glad I get to have both." My gaze flits from Kaylee to Braxton. "But more than that, I'm glad I get to stay here with you guys."

Kaylee grins. "Ditto."

"They're coming by the studio tomorrow to watch us practice."

"Good." Kaylee smiles softly. "You deserve this second chance,

Gage. You've worked hard to get to this point."

Wanting to give them their space, I head to my room, where I spend the rest of the night looking for homes in the 'burbs. I might deserve a second chance at finding love and happiness, but I don't deserve Sadie possibly giving us a chance, not after the shit I pulled back when I was high and hell-bent on destroying everything good in my life. On the other hand, she deserves the entire world, and I'm going to make sure I give it to her.

Twenty

Sadie

Gage: Are you still coming by?

I GLANCE AT THE TIME AND SIGH IN EXHAUSTION. RORY WAS UP HALF THE NIGHT IN TEARS over a tooth coming in, and since I didn't bring any of her medicine with me, I had nothing to help with the pain. I could've called Gage and asked him to pick something up, but I kept telling myself she would calm down soon. She finally passed out from exhaustion a couple of hours ago, and I'm not too keen on waking her up.

Me: Rory had trouble sleeping last night and is still sleeping. I don't think it's going to happen. Rain check?

I feel horrible that I had to cancel on him the first time he invited us to the studio, but everyone with kids knows parenting rule number one: never wake a sleeping baby.

Gage: Is she okay? Do you need anything? I can come over.

My heart warms at how devoted he is to being a good dad. I

would be lying if I said a part of me wasn't scared to let him in, especially after our past, but so far, he hasn't once made me regret it, and while the self-preservation part of me wants to run and hide, the adult in me, who's been through hell and back, knows that even though life can be scary as hell, it can also be taken from you at any minute. Which means I'm pretty much stuck somewhere between wanting to live life to the fullest with no regrets and not making the same mistakes that have already cost me everything once before. Yeah, it's as exhausting and complicated and confusing as it sounds.

Me: Thank you, but we're okay. I'm going to attempt to get a nap in while she's sleeping, and then I'm supposed to meet Kendall later regarding the condo. Have a good practice.

I've just set my phone on the table and have swung my legs onto the couch when a cry comes from the bedroom, followed by "Mama!"

"Good morning," I say, walking into her temporary room and finding her standing in her crib, bouncing up and down.

"Ow, ow!" she squeals. Since she's not crying, I assume she's trying to say *out*. It amazes me every day how fast she's growing and learning. After losing Collin, it makes me appreciate Rory and every milestone that much more. Sometimes, I see little similarities in how they smile and laugh, and it makes me both happy and sad to see pieces of Collin living through her.

"Well, since you're awake, want to go see Daddy?" I ask, lifting her out of her crib and setting her on the bed to change her diaper since there's no changing table here.

"Dada!" She giggles, clearly happier than she was last night.

"Okay, we'll go see Daddy."

On the way to the studio, Kendall texts me that she has an appointment, but can meet tomorrow, if that's okay. As much as I hate being stuck in a hotel, she's doing me a huge favor, and it'll be quicker than me finding a place, so I agree without complaint. Even once I see the condo, I'm still going to have to deal with hiring a moving company to have all our stuff moved here. Since I was renting month to month, I'll at least be able to give notice and cancel the lease next month.

When we arrive, Easton stands by the front desk and greets us, offering to walk us back to the studio where the guys are practicing. We slip into what Easton refers to as the control room, and he ensures me that if Rory makes any noise, the guys won't be affected or disturbed.

The second we walk inside, the music hits our ears. From listening to their earlier albums, I know that while they're a rock band, they're on the calmer side—less screaming, more passion—giving off a Fallout Boy meets Matchbox Twenty vibe. My dad was a huge music buff, and I grew up listening to all types of old-school music.

The thought of my dad causes a dull ache in my chest. My parents tried for years to have a baby, but it wasn't until my mom was forty-seven and my dad was fifty-three that she mistakenly got pregnant with me. They were so excited but also scared because of her age. Everything turned out okay, but them having me later in life meant I didn't have any siblings. I also lost them in my early twenties, shortly after I got married and gave birth to Collin.

I glance out at the band, zeroing in on Gage, remembering what Kaylee said about him being an orphan and the only family he has is his band. A deep sense of understanding tugs at my heartstrings. In a lot of ways, we're both alone in this world, seeking love and acceptance, a safe place to land when we fall, and if I let Gage in, we can be each other's soft landing.

"All right, that was good," Camden says. His gaze meets mine, and he nods subtly. I expect him to tell Gage I'm here, but instead, he says, "Let's do 'Bleeding Heart' next." The guys nod, and then Gage, who's sitting behind his drum kit, counts them in and then starts. I don't know anything about music, but holy shit, the way he hits the drums wakes up something in me that's been dormant for a long time. I don't know if it's the passion in his eyes or the way his muscular forearms and biceps flex every time he hits the drums, but damn, it's suddenly hot in here.

Declan and Braxton both join in with their guitars, and a second later, Camden starts singing. His eyes meet mine once again, and as he sings the first line, he winks at me. At first, I wonder what the hell is going on until Easton murmurs, "Gage wrote this song," and then it all clicks.

Emerald eyes, soft smile, big heart
She's everything a man could ever want
Makes it bittersweet to know there's a chance
She'll never be mine
Someone like me doesn't deserve her time
But that doesn't stop me from wanting to take what's mine
From wanting her heart to be mine
Her body, her soul, all mine

So I'm holding on, biding my time
Waiting for the chance
To prove I'm worth her time
She captured my heart
Broken, bleeding
It was useless, barely beating
But with one look, one touch, she brought me back to life
Now I'm living, breathing
Every day I'm healing

And I want the same for her
I want to be the one for her

It won't be easy, but I'm determined to heal her bleeding heart
She's got no reason to let me in
To give me the chance to make shit right
But I'm not going to stop
Until I've reached into her chest and taken hold of her broken heart
It's bleeding crimson all over the floor
But I'm going to heal it, fix the broken, and bring her back to life
So she's living, breathing, feeling what she does to me

So I'm holding on, biding my time
Waiting for the chance
To prove I'm worth her time
She captured my heart
Broken, bleeding
It was useless, barely beating
But with one look, one touch, she brought me back to life
Now I'm living, breathing
Every day I'm healing
And I want the same for her
I want to be the one for her

By the time the song ends, tears trail down my cheeks like twin waterfalls, knowing that song was about me.

And if I didn't already know, when Gage's eyes connect with mine, raw emotion etched in his features, it's confirmed.

Camden tells the guys they're done practicing for the day, but Gage is already heading our way. I don't know where Easton and the guy working the sound booth went, but when Gage walks in, it's only him, Rory, and me.

"I thought you weren't coming..."

"Rory woke up." I shrug, trying to play off the fact that my body buzzes with electricity, and my heart feels like it's been resuscitated. "You wrote that song for me."

Gage grins. "I did."

He steps closer, his hand about to touch somewhere on me when Rory shrieks, "Dada, ow!"

His attention turns on her. "What's wrong?" He bends so he's at her level.

"Ow! Ow!"

"Sadie, is she okay?" he asks, worry in his tone as he unsnaps her straps and lifts her into his arms. The second she's out of her stroller, she claps, a huge smile spreading across her face.

"I think she's learned a new word," I say with a laugh. "Ow seems to be *out*, only she can't say the t yet."

Gage sighs in relief, smiling at his daughter. "Is that what you wanted, princess? To get out of your stroller?" She presses her hands to the sides of his face and smushes his cheeks together. "Dada!"

"I'm so glad you guys are here," he says, kissing the tip of her nose and making her giggle. "Have you heard from Kendall?"

"She had to reschedule. I think we're going to meet up tomorrow." I shrug. "But on the positive, it means we're free for the rest of the day."

Gage grins. "What do you say we go get something to eat and take it to the park?"

"That sounds perfect."

After saying bye to the guys, we take off. Since the park Gage wants to go to is a bit of a ways away, we throw the stroller in the trunk and have Paul—Gage's main bodyguard—drive us to grab the food.

We stop at a deli that Gage swears is the best in New York. Since they're old-school with no online menu or ordering, we get out so I can check out what they have.

We're walking across the sidewalk, with Paul behind us, when a woman says Gage's name, making both of us look her way. She's too old to be a fan—at least not one who would fangirl over him—so it must be someone he knows.

"Sandra," Gage clips.

Her gaze bounces between Gage, Rory, and me, landing and staying on me. "I'm sorry. You just... you look so much like my Tori..."

"Don't you fucking mention her name," Gage snaps, stepping in her face. "And when you see me on the streets, you don't approach me, ever."

"I'm sorry... I..."

"I don't give a shit," he says, his words coming out so cold that a chill races up my spine. Without waiting for her to respond, he takes my hand and pulls me into the deli. We order our food, the tension thick, and then head to the park, stopping once along the way for Paul to run in and grab us a blanket.

When we arrive at the park, one I've never been to before, it's quiet with only a few people meandering about. We walk for a while, looking for a good spot.

"How about here?" Gage asks, pointing at a shaded area under a big tree that's not too far from the playground. While he lays the blanket out, I cover Rory with her blanket since it's cool outside and she's fallen asleep in her stroller.

We eat in silence, and the entire time I can't stop thinking about what that woman said—that I look like her daughter. If that's true, is that why Gage is attracted to me? Am I a weird replacement for the woman he lost all those years ago? I can't imagine that's a healthy coping mechanism.

When the silence—and tension—gets to be too much, I open my mouth to ask about what happened, but before I can get a word out, Gage speaks.

"You both have red hair and green eyes, but that's where the similarities end. Tori's mom was always good at playing games, and I have no doubt that she was playing games when she said that bullshit. She might've looked like a grief-stricken mom, but she knew her husband was sexually molesting and raping her daughter, and she chose to ignore it."

"She knew?" I breathe, my eyes going to a still sleeping Rory, unable to fathom how a mother could ever know that her child was being raped and do nothing about it. A monster like that deserves to burn in hell... they both do. "Are you sure?"

Gage nods. "Yeah, Tori wrote me a note before she ended her life. After she died and I read it, I went after her mom and stepdad. She knew and chose not to believe her."

"Did he pay?"

"Kind of." Gage swallows thickly. "I went after them, specifically him, saying I would expose him to the world. He was a cocky bastard and didn't take me seriously, saying he would destroy my credibility and reputation, ending my music career before it even started.

"Easton overheard and forced me to get on a plane to LA. He said to let him handle it, that he would make sure he pays, but I would regret it if the last thing everyone remembered about Tori was that she was a rape victim." Gage's eyes glisten, and I find myself gravitating toward him, taking his hand in mine and threading our fingers together.

He glances down and smiles sadly, then brings our joined hands to his mouth, pressing a soft kiss to my hand. "As much as I wanted to expose him to the world, I agreed. Tori deserved more than to have her memory tainted. It was his word versus hers, and she wasn't alive to fight back. So I got on the plane and trusted Easton to handle it. A few days later, Glen... that's her stepdad's name... killed himself."

"Well, if that doesn't prove his guilt..."

"Yeah," he agrees. "It sucks that nobody will ever know what he did to her but knowing that he's been permanently removed from the earth and will never hurt anyone else again and that Tori's mom is now alone and has to live with the guilt of knowing she didn't do shit when her daughter went to her and begged her to listen is a decent consolation."

"Rory will always know she can talk to us," I tell him, feeling like he needs to hear that.

He nods, half with me and half lost in his thoughts. "Yeah, we'll make sure of that."

After a few minutes, he circles back to the initial topic. "Tori was beautiful, with red hair and green eyes. She was wild and carefree." A small half-smile forms on his lips. "But she was young. We both were... She loved to smoke and drink and had a reckless streak to her. I loved her the only way a teenage boy could, and after she died, that love morphed into guilt."

His eyes meet mine. "When I saw you crying at the cemetery, my mind went to Tori, not because of your looks, but because when our eyes collided, I saw in you what I often saw in her: devastation. You were so damn sad and lost, and that's what drew you to me. I couldn't save Tori, so I wanted to save you."

Gage laughs humorlessly. "Fuck, I couldn't even save myself."

"Stop," I say, moving closer to him. "When I had no one, you were there. When I landed myself in jail, you were there. And when I couldn't go home, you gave me a safe place to stay until I could function again."

"And then I pushed you out the door by fucking two women," he growls, shaking his head and moving back slightly, so we're no longer connected.

"I need you to know, no matter how slow you want to go, I'm okay with that. Just the fact you're giving us a chance means the world to me. I'll do whatever it takes to make you trust me again, to show you that you're all I want and that you mean the world to me." His gaze sears into mine, pleading with me to know he means every word he's saying.

"It is hard," I admit. "Sometimes, when I would think about you, the memory of you with them appears, and it hurts. But I won't be that woman who throws your past in your face. You're clean and working hard to have a fresh start, and it's not fair for me to bring up what you did while you were high. But you're right, I do need for us to take things slow, so I can protect my heart."

Gage nods in understanding, framing my face with his hand. "One day, you're going to trust me with your heart." He leans in and brushes his lips against mine. The act is soft and sweet as if he's showing me that he can go slow and take things at the pace I need.

"I promise you, Sadie," he murmurs against my mouth, "when you're ready to give me your heart, I'm going to protect it and keep it safe." He gently sucks my bottom lip into his mouth, and butterflies erupt in my belly.

And as I kiss Gage back, I feel the truth in the lyrics he wrote for me—slowly, with every word, every promise, every action, he's bringing me back to life.

Twenty-One
Gage

"THIS IS TOO MUCH." SADIE SCANS THE ROOM WITH WIDE EYES, TAKING IN THE SPACIOUS living room and kitchen. She follows Kendall down the hallway and gasps when she sees the master bedroom completely furnished. "I can't accept this." Kendall ignores her, showing her the second bedroom that's also furnished, complete with a crib, changing table, and dresser. "Nope, I can't do it." She cuts in front of Kendall before she can continue with the tour. "Did you hear me? This is too much. I can't move in here… accept all of this, and I can't even imagine how much it all cost."

"You can and you will," Kendall says. "You being here means Gage gets to remain in the band, the band my husband is part of. Heck, it means there's still a band because everyone knows those guys were not going to record without Gage. This"—she waves her hand in the air—"is the least I can do, and I'm only supplying the condo. Gage bought all the furniture."

Sadie's eyes land on me. "Gage." She sighs. "You didn't have to do this."

I shrug, not wanting to point out that her furniture was all cheaply made and that she and Rory deserve the best of everything. She provided a beautiful, loving home for our daughter, and that's all that matters, but since I'm able to give them the best, I'm going to damn well do so. Money doesn't mean shit to me, but her happiness does.

"Wait a second," she says, walking over to the dresser where there's a picture frame with a photo of Collin and Sadie. She put it on the dresser so Rory would grow up, knowing about the brother she never got to meet. "How did this get here?"

"All your stuff is here," I tell her. "I left your stuff in boxes in your closet, figuring you would want to go through them yourself, but I set up everything else. I didn't want you to have to deal with all of that with a toddler in tow. The place is move-in ready."

Sadie's eyes soften. She's been in the hotel for almost a week now, assuming Kendall was too busy to meet her to show her the place while we were getting everything ready. Not once did Sadie complain, though, when I know it was rough living in a shared space with an almost one-year-old. Speaking of which, with Rory's birthday coming up, I should ask Sadie how she wants to go about celebrating.

"Thank you," she says, hugging me tightly and nestling her face into my neck.

Kendall waggles her brows and mouths, "*You did good,*" before quietly exiting so we can have some privacy. Rory is with Layla since Sadie assumed the place would need to be cleaned before attempting to move in. Over the past week, while the guys and I have been practicing, Layla, Kendall, and Kendall's sister, Bailey, welcomed Sadie into their little mom circle

At first, Sadie was nervous and a bit overwhelmed, but after their first playdate—where the women had what they call a Mommy

Meeting, which includes drinking wine and gossiping—she was excited to have made new friends while Rory played with the other kids. I learned from Declan that Sadie's been fantasizing about my pierced cock—and Kendall and Layla tried to convince their husbands to get pierced as well—she met me back at the hotel all smiles. The next day she joined them at the park, and the day after, they all met at that indoor playground. It means a lot to me that she gave my friends a chance and gels so seamlessly with them.

"Where's Kendall?" Sadie asks when she pulls back and realizes that we're alone.

"She left."

Sadie pouts. "I wanted to say thank you."

"You can tomorrow. We're going over to their house for a barbecue."

Her eyes meet mine, and a soft smile curves at the corners of her lips. "Does that mean we're alone?"

"It does," I say, unsure where she's going with this until a tiny twinkle fills her gaze, and she steps on her tiptoes to press her mouth to mine.

"That means I can thank you properly," she murmurs against my lips. Every night, after I'm done at practice, I've been going over to the hotel to hang out with Sadie and Rory. While Rory's awake, our focus is on her, playing and eating dinner, running through her bedtime routine, but once she's asleep, Sadie and I get alone time.

We spend the majority of the time talking and getting to know one another, but for the past couple of days, we've split our time between talking and kissing. I can't remember the last time I simply kissed a woman—for so long, I resorted to fucking, keeping any and all emotion out of the act—but I have to admit, kissing Sadie has become one of my favorite pastimes. Her lips are soft and pouty and when she sighs into the kiss, my cock twitches, loving the sound as much as I do.

"You don't need to thank me," I mutter. "But I sure as hell won't stop you from kissing me."

Our mouths connect, our tongues gliding along each other, and I revel in her sweet taste as I lift her into my arms, carrying her out of Rory's room and back into the living room. I go to set her on the couch next to me, but her legs lock around my waist, and she remains on my lap when I sit down. Every time we kiss, I let her control the situation, not wanting to go faster than she's ready for. She deserves my patience and for us to take each step at her pace.

With her straddling my lap, she deepens the kiss, running her fingers through my hair and fisting the strands, silently demanding more. I break the kiss, trailing fiery kisses along her neck, suckling on her soft flesh, reacquainting myself with every inch of her, memorizing every freckle and beauty mark. When we were together before, I was too high to appreciate what I had, but now that I'm sober, I refuse to take any part of her for granted.

"Oh, God," she breathes when I suck on the sensitive spot just under her ear, no doubt leaving a mark. Her center grinds down on my crotch, and I slide my hands down her hips and cup her pert ass, loving the way her soft body feels against my own.

She releases my hair and lifts her shirt over her head, exposing a black lace bra that shows off the swells of her breasts and hardened nipples.

Not wanting to assume anything, I meet her eyes. "May I?" I ask, praying to God she doesn't say no.

"So polite." She smirks. Leaning forward, she sucks my bottom lip into her mouth, nipping at it playfully. "Yes, Gage, you may touch me."

Not needing to be told twice, I take her lace-covered breast in my palm and suck on her nipple through the material. She groans, her fingers spearing through my hair again as I take her other breast and suck on that one too.

After giving them each attention, I pull back and flip the cup down to get a good look at her. Her breasts are creamy like the rest of her body, with tiny freckles dotting her skin. She mentioned her mom was Irish, and she took after her. With her tits nestled in my hands, I lick her pink nipples, my tongue swirling around the tip before I bite down on them.

Sadie groans, jutting her chest toward me. "More," she breathes.

I lick her nipples again, but she shakes her head. "No, not that… umm…"

"What, baby? What do you want?"

Her pale skin flushes pink, telling me she's embarrassed by whatever she's trying to say, so I drop her tits and take her face in my hands. "You never have to be embarrassed by what you want. Whatever it is, I'll give it to you."

She sucks her bottom lip into her mouth and nods slowly. "I want you to bite me again. When we were together before, you would do that. And sometimes, you would be kind of rough. I never thought I would like sex like that, but I do."

Fuck, this woman.

Capturing her mouth with mine, I kiss her hard and deep, stroking my tongue against hers. Needing her to know, to *feel* how badly I fucking want her. I pull back slightly and lick across her bottom lip before I bite down on it… *hard*, making her groan into my mouth.

Releasing her, I grab her tits again, this time less gentle, and take a nipple into my mouth, sucking roughly on the tip.

"Oh, yes, just like that," she murmurs, throwing her head back and grinding herself against my hard cock. If she keeps doing that, she's going to get us both off.

The harder I suck and bite, the harder she grinds against me, stroking my dick through the material while taking us closer to the edge.

"Oh, oh, God," she breathes, telling me that she's close. Her thighs tighten, and I have no doubt she's about to come when my phone rings in my pocket, making us both stop. I want nothing more than to ignore it, but with Rory at Camden and Layla's, I can't chance it's her, and something's wrong.

When I voice my thoughts, lifting Sadie off my lap—leaving us both unsatisfied—so I can grab my phone, she nods in agreement.

Sure enough, it's Layla.

"Hey, is everything okay?" I ask, wincing when my words come out sounding all breathy like I was just in the middle of a hot as hell sex session.

"Hey," she says slowly, clearly picking up on my vibe. "Sorry to bother you. Everything's okay, but I think Marianna has an ear infection, so I need to take her to the pediatrician. Camden can watch her, but I just wanted to check with you guys first."

"Nah, it's all good," I say, standing. "I'll come get her right now."

"You sure?"

I glance down at Sadie, who's still without a shirt, looking up at me with a mixture of heat and concern. "Yeah."

"What happened?" Sadie asks, her voice as out of breath as mine.

"Marianna has an ear infection, so Layla needs to take her to the doctor. Why don't you stay here and start unpacking your boxes, and I'll go pick up Rory and grab us some dinner?"

We talked about me announcing that I have a daughter, but I haven't posted anything yet in my attempt to take shit slow. I've been keeping our relationship a secret from the world, which means, aside from the picnic at the park, we've been spending our time behind closed doors in her hotel room.

Sadie's entire body visibly stiffens, and I wonder what I said wrong until I replay my words in my head. She's afraid of me picking up Rory… of driving with her. Of me being high and getting both of us killed. I want to be offended that after a year of me being clean and weeks of showing her that I wouldn't risk Rory's life, she would still think like that, but I can't be because she told me she needs to take things slow, and I have to give it to her. After what she's been through, I'm not sure she'll ever fully trust me, but I'm going to work every day to earn it.

"Paul will drive us," I add, texting Paul to pick me up.

"Oh, okay." She leans over and kisses me softly. "Thank you… for understanding."

"One day at a time," I tell her, kissing her back, knowing that even me going with Paul without her is a big deal and a show of trust.

I'm waiting for Paul to arrive when I reach into my pocket to get my phone and realize I've forgotten it. I must've left it on the table, and there's no way I'm going to get Rory without Sadie being able to get ahold of me. I run back upstairs to grab it and let myself in, so I can run in and out without bothering Sadie, but when I get inside, I hear a noise coming from somewhere in the condo.

Concerned something might be wrong, I head down the hall, following the noise. The door to the bedroom is shut, so I knock. "Sadie!"

I hear, "Oh, shit," which has me opening the door, thinking something is wrong before she can finish telling me to wait. "You okay?" I ask, finding her lying on the bed.

"Yep," she squeaks out, sounding all kinds of weird.

I glance around, wondering what's going on, when I hear a buzzing sound. "Do you hear that?" I step closer.

"Nope, don't you need to go get Rory? You should go get her…

Don't want to make Layla wait."

The way she's talking a million miles a second has me walking into the room, confused and curious. "You don't hear that noise?" I ask, ignoring her comment.

"I said, I don't."

I'm now next to the bed, and the noise is loud as fuck. There's no way she doesn't hear it… I drop onto my hands and knees since it sounds like it's coming from under the bed, and she screeches, "Stop!" as she leaps toward me, damn near jumping on my back.

Realizing the noise is coming from the drawer and not under the bed, I pull it open and find a dark pink-looking rose thing… vibrating.

"What the hell is this?" I ask, lifting it.

"Oh, my God, Gage! Give it to me," Sadie shrieks, trying to snatch it from me. "It's mine!"

And that's when it clicks—Sadie on the bed, acting weird, begging me to leave, sounding guilty and now embarrassed. The vibration is a goddamn vibrator, and I just walked in on her about to get herself off.

"It won't turn off," she mutters. "I think I've overused it." She covers her face with her hands, making me chuckle.

"Hey," I say, removing her hands. "You don't need to hide anything from me. Besides, the thought of you lying in this bed, fingering yourself, is sexy as hell."

"I wasn't fingering myself. It's a clit stimulator."

"Oh, yeah?" I glance down at it and notice it's the shape of a rose, and the center is what's vibrating. "Show me how it works."

Her eyes go wide. "What? No!" She shakes her head at the same time as I nod mine.

"Yes." I grab her legs and pull her down the bed to lie on her back with her head propped up by the pillows. Since her clothes are still on, I'm assuming she must've pulled her shorts and panties to the side to use it, but I'm not having it, so I yank them down her legs, exposing her neatly trimmed pussy and creamy thighs.

My phone is going off somewhere in the house, but I ignore it. Paul can fucking wait, and Camden can keep an eye on Rory for a few minutes while I get my woman off.

"Spread your thighs, baby."

Despite her initial protest, she does as I say, giving me the perfect view of her glistening pussy. Between our dry humping and her using the toy, she must be so damn wet. I lift the still vibrating rose thing to my nose and inhale. "Fuck, Sadie, I can smell your juices on this thing."

She groans, her eyes turning hooded.

"Show me how it works," I repeat, handing it to her.

She takes the vibrating rose from me and slowly puts it between her legs, nestling it against her pretty pink pussy. The moment it touches her clit, she shivers in anticipation, and I want nothing more than to replace that plastic shit with my tongue. I've never been jealous of an inanimate object until now.

"Were you thinking about me when you had this between your legs?" I ask, lying on my stomach and giving the inside of her thigh a kiss.

She nods, her chest rising and falling in quick succession.

"What were you thinking about? Tell me."

"I was thinking…" She swallows thickly. "I was thinking about how much I want you. I was imagining the rose was your mouth, licking me." She moans softly, the toy bringing her closer to her climax.

"Oh, shit," she breathes, her lust-filled eyes meeting mine. "I'm so close."

Having had enough of that toy bringing her the pleasure I want for myself, I pull the toy away and chuck it to the side, the damn thing still vibrating like crazy.

"Gage! What the—?"

Pushing her thighs apart, I dip down and lick my way slowly up her slit, causing her words to turn into a needy groan.

"Mine," I growl, taking her clit between my lips and sucking on the swollen nub. "Tell me this pussy is mine."

"Oh, God. Yes, it's yours," she breathes as I lay my tongue flat on the sensitive area and begin massaging circles, working her up the same way that toy was. The only difference is that, like this, I get to taste her juices and feel her body shaking in pleasure. I work her up higher and higher until she explodes around my tongue, coating me with her orgasm. I don't stop, wanting every bit of her desire until she's pushing my head away.

"That was way better than my rose," she admits, her tone relaxed and sated.

I crawl up her body and kiss her. I expect her to pull back since my mouth is coated with her pleasure, but instead, she licks the seam of my lips and moans. My dick swells in my pants at the sound, wanting to join the fun, but I push the thought aside because we're taking shit slow.

My phone rings in the background, and with one more quick kiss, I get off her, grabbing the toy and pressing the power button several times until it finally stops vibrating.

"Oh, thank God," she mutters. "That thing is getting thrown in the garbage."

I laugh, tossing it at her.

"Ewww, Gage!"

"What? It's your juices." I lick my lips, and she rolls her eyes. "Paul's waiting for me. I forgot my phone. I'll be back soon."

"Or… we could go together," she suggests. "Go out to dinner."

"We'd be seen together," I point out, "and nobody knows about you guys yet."

"So you can tell them. Post it while we're on our way." She crawls over to me and wraps her arms around me, still naked from the waist down. "Rory's your daughter, and I'm your girlfriend. I don't want us to be a secret. If you want people to know, I'm okay with that."

"You're sure?" I ask, loving that she used the word girlfriend to describe what she is to me. "Once we do this, there's no going back. No matter what happens, it will all be in the public eye."

"I'm sure." She presses her lips to mine. "I trust you to make sure we're protected."

And just like that, with that one sentence, I fall even harder for the woman in my arms. She has every reason not to trust me, yet here she is, slowly giving me her trust. As I look into her vulnerable green eyes, I vow to never break that trust.

"All right, let's do this."

Twenty-Two

Sadie

AS PAUL DRIVES US TO PICK UP RORY, GAGE GOES OVER WHAT HE'S GOING TO POST ON social media with Bailey—who's in charge of Blackwood's social media—and my thoughts drift to the past hour. How we explored my new home. Things getting heated with Gage until the moment was cut short because Rory needed to be picked up. Gage walking in and taking over when I was attempting to finish what we started.

After he made me come, I thought he would try to take the next step and have sex. I wasn't sure how I would react, afraid the flashbacks and memories of him being with those other women would hit. Until the moment came when I orgasmed, and then he pulled back, not even trying for more. I didn't have a single thought about our past, not a flash of what happened the night he pushed me away, and it made me realize that I'm ready to move forward with Gage. I was just as shocked as he was when I referred to myself as his girlfriend, but I must admit that it felt right when the word came out. Being with Gage *feels* right.

He's spent the past month and a half showing me every day how much he's changed and how important Rory and I are to him. Two of the days after practice, he texted to let me know he was going to a meeting before coming over, extending an invitation to join him when I'm ready. He said he doesn't want to keep the two worlds separate, that his recovery is a part of his life and will always be, and he wants us to be a part of that. I never got that from Vincent, and I know now it's because he wasn't really trying to get clean. He was lying, putting on a front, and hiding shit, but Gage... he's up front about everything. And that makes me want to take the next step with him.

"Is this okay?" Gage asks, handing me his phone. As I read the statement he typed up—stating that after the past sixteen months of working on himself, getting clean, and fighting every day to stay that way, he's back, and with him is his daughter and girlfriend—tears fill my eyes. While meant to be positive and uplifting, his words are a harsh reminder that if Gage had been successful at taking his life, we wouldn't be here. Rory never would've gotten to meet her dad, and Gage and I wouldn't be getting this second chance. The statement is accompanied by a selfie we took while at the park with Rory. We're smiling at the camera with her in the middle.

"Promise me something," I tell him, turning to look him in the eyes. "Promise me that no matter what happens between us, no matter where life takes us, you will always fight for your life. Rory needs her daddy. She needs him to be clean and *alive*. And..." I choke up, my emotions getting the best of me. "I need you too. Even if we don't work out, I need you as Rory's dad."

Gage reaches out and swipes my falling tears. "I promise, Sadie, I'm never going back to being that shell of a man again. I love my life. I love my daughter, and I'm falling in love with you. And no drug is worth the risk of losing you guys."

I sigh in relief as he pulls me into a hug. "I know you're scared," he murmurs into my ear. "And you have every right to be, but I promise, I'm here, I'm clean, and I'm going to fight every day to stay that way. Not just for you guys but for me too."

He holds me tight for several long beats before he backs up and looks at me, his eyes glassy with emotion. "We got this… one day at a time."

He posts it, and within seconds, comments and likes start flooding his notifications. "I haven't posted in over two years," he says with a nervous laugh, scrolling through the feed. I can't read them all, but the ones I catch are sweet, welcoming him back and congratulating him on becoming a dad. A few are from women asking to have his baby and wanting to screw him, but I refuse to let those bother me. I'm not oblivious to the fact that Gage is more than hot and has been Raging Chaos's *bad boy* for years, doing drugs, partying, and having sex with women he didn't bother to get to know. But that Gage isn't the man sitting next to me, and maybe it makes me foolish or naïve, but until Gage proves otherwise, I'm trusting him to be the man he is now.

"All right, well, I've had enough of that," he says, swiping out of the app and pocketing his phone. "Let's go get our princess and have our first family dinner in public."

OUR FIRST PUBLIC FAMILY DINNER IS AT A LATTE FUN, WHERE WE SPEND HOURS PLAYING with Rory. Gage jumps on the trampoline with her, goes down the slide with her in his lap a couple dozen times, swims through the ball pit, and shows her how to draw with chalk all over the chalkboard wall. And when our little angel turns into the devil at dinnertime, he never once loses his patience as he gently calms her until her cries turn into giggles.

Once we've eaten and Rory is back in her stroller, we stroll downtown with Paul lingering behind. Gage said he doesn't bring Paul everywhere he goes in New York, but he doesn't want to take a chance with us—better safe than sorry.

"What the hell is that?" Gage asks when we stop in front of the Easter Bunny.

"The Easter Bunny," I say with a laugh. "Tomorrow is Easter, hence the reason for the barbecue at Kendall and Declan's place."

"Do you celebrate Easter?"

"Yeah, I mean, I did when Collin was alive. I'm not super religious. We didn't go to church or anything, but we'd celebrate all the major holidays like Easter and Christmas." I shrug, a lump of emotion clogging my throat. "Rory's not old enough to understand, but once she's a little older, the Easter Bunny will bring her a basket, and Santa will bring her presents."

Gage nods toward where the bunny is sitting. "It looks like people are getting their pictures taken with it. Want to get Rory's taken?"

"Sure. She's not really dressed for it, but I guess it doesn't matter."

The line isn't long, so we only have to wait a few minutes before it's our turn. Gage pulls Rory out of her stroller and walks over to the bunny, who extends his arms to place her in his lap. Rory isn't having it, though, and latches onto Gage like he's an extension of her.

"I think I'll just sit next to you," Gage says, keeping hold of his daughter, who doesn't appear impressed by the bunny in the slightest.

I step back to take a couple of pictures of them when an overwhelming sense of déjà vu hits me. I try to shake it off, snapping photo after photo, but it's too strong and threatens to take me under.

"Join us, Sadie," Gage says, calling me over.

"I can take your picture," the photographer adds.

I have a seat on the other side of the bunny, and the photographer tells us to smile, snapping a picture, but something feels off, and that's when it hits me.

I was here before… with Collin.

Once we're done, the photographer gives us a ticket so we can go to the counter and purchase the photo. The woman takes the ticket and scans it, and our photo pops up on the screen. Only instead of seeing Gage, Rory, and me, my brain changes it to Collin and the bunny. The image knocks me back a couple of steps, and I bump into Gage. Thankfully, Rory is in her stroller, and Gage catches me before we hit the ground.

"Are you okay?" he asks, his voice filled with concern.

"I…" Images of Collin running to the Easter Bunny, smiling for the camera, and then hugging him take over my brain, making it hard to think, speak, *breathe*. My little boy… He's gone. He'll never experience another holiday again. No more bunnies or Santas… He'll never open another present or look for hidden eggs.

"Oh, my God, are you Gage Sharp?" a woman says. "I am a huge fan. Oh! And you must be his girlfriend. I saw the post on Instagram."

She continues to fangirl, but all I can focus on is trying to keep my shit together. But the thoughts and images hit me like a freight train, and the next thing I know, everything goes black.

"SADIE," GAGE SAYS SOFTLY. "WAKE UP, BABY."

I wrench my lids open and find I'm lying on a couch in a room I've never seen before. "What happened?" I croak, trying to sit up. The room spins, so I close my eyes for a few moments before opening them again.

"I think you had a panic attack and passed out," Gage says.

"I took Collin to see that Easter Bunny."

"Oh, baby." He wraps his arms around me. "I'm so sorry."

"It's not your fault. I forgot until you guys sat down, and then it hit me. It's been almost two years, and it still hurts so much," I choke out.

"Mama," Rory says softly, using a tone she rarely uses.

"Paul grabbed her and the stroller so I could carry you into the office," Gage says.

"Mama," Rory repeats, reaching out for me. She's too young to understand, but babies can sense when something is off.

"Hey, sweet girl." I lift her out of her stroller and hug her tightly, needing to smell her baby scent and feel her heartbeat.

"Did that fan see me pass out?" I ask, flinching at the thought of someone getting it on camera.

"Nah, I signed something for her, and she took off before you blacked out. The manager saw it all go down and opened the office for us to get you out of the public eye. But even if she did, the only thing that matters is that you're okay."

"God, I can't believe I did that," I mutter. "What if you weren't with us, and it was just Rory and me?"

Gage cups the back of my neck and turns my face to look at him. "You're the strongest woman I know, but sometimes it's okay to be weak. You've been through more shit than most people, and thinking about what-ifs won't do you any good. I was here... I *am* here."

"I miss him so much," I admit softly. "Every second of every day.

Sometimes, without realizing it, my guilt hits. Like with the Easter Bunny… Collin will never have that experience again. And here I am, living my life, taking Rory to see the Easter Bunny, laughing and making new memories while he's buried in a cemetery. I know my thoughts are irrational—"

"Hell no, they're not," he says. "Your thoughts are what drove me to drugs. The guilt I felt over losing her, over not being able to save her. I know we talked about you meeting with Viola for me, but have you considered talking to someone on your own?"

"What is that supposed to mean?" I ask, pulling back and out of his reach. "I'm not going to turn to drugs." Sure, I had my moments, but I got through the roughest part and made it to the other side.

"I didn't say you were." He sighs, and I instantly feel bad for snapping at him. "I was just trying to say that I understand and can relate, and maybe talking to someone will help. You've been through a lot and haven't spoken to anyone about it."

He makes a valid point, and while I'm doing okay, for the most part, having a panic attack and blacking out from a memory is probably something worth speaking to someone about. Especially since it's happened before—thankfully before Rory was born and only once afterward, while she was sleeping.

"You're right," I concede. "I'm going to talk to someone. It can't hurt, right?" I drop my head to his shoulder. "Aren't we quite the pair?"

Gage chuckles. "Hell yeah, we are."

Since the manager had the photo printed for us, we're able to leave through the back door so we don't risk being seen. It's getting late, so we drive straight to the condo after Gage lets me know that he had someone pack up all our stuff in the hotel room and check us out. I should probably be a bit annoyed that he's packed up and moved my stuff twice now without my consent, but I'm too appreciative to question it.

When we get inside, Gage insists I take a bath to relax while he gives Rory one. My nerves are still a bit rattled, so I take him up on his offer and use the time to unwind, meeting him back in Rory's room as he's finishing her bedtime story. She's already fast asleep, so I give her a soft kiss, not wanting to wake her up.

"How are you feeling?" Gage asks, sitting on the couch and pulling me onto his lap.

"Better." I snuggle into his chest. "Today was really nice… aside from me blacking out."

"Yeah, it was." He kisses the top of my head. "But that bunny was creepy as fuck, Sadie. You sure you didn't black out from that?"

Appreciating his attempt to lighten the mood with a joke, I laugh into his chest. "He's not creepy. He's a cute little bunny."

"Babe, he's the shit nightmares are made of. Did you see how Rory reacted? Even she recognized the creepy vibes. And who in the hell decided to make it a normal thing where animals sit on benches and kids sit on their laps?" He mock shivers. "Are there other scary animals I should be aware of?"

"No," I say, sitting up with a laugh and playfully slapping his arm. "But there is Santa."

"Oh fuck, I forgot about him," Gage groans. "I think we need to start a new tradition. One that doesn't involve our daughter sitting on creepy-ass men's laps and taking photos with them."

I wrap my arms around Gage's neck. "What about me? Can I sit on creepy-ass men's laps and take photos with them?"

"Fuck no," Gage growls, gripping the curves of my hips and pulling me closer to him. "The only lap you're sitting on is mine."

His mouth crashes against mine, and all thoughts of the Easter Bunny and Santa and blacking out go straight out the window as I get lost in everything that is Gage.

"Stay the night," I murmur against his lips.

"You sure?" he asks, breaking the kiss and resting his forehead against mine.

"I want you to spend the night… in my bed." My eyes lock with his as I grind down on his hard crotch. "I want to finish what we started earlier today."

Twenty-Three

Sadie

GAGE DROPS ME ONTO THE CENTER OF THE BED AND THEN BACKS UP, REACHING BEHIND him and lifting his T-shirt over his head, exposing his tattooed chest and six-pack abs. When we were together before, I never took the time to appreciate his body, too lost in my grief, and because of the drugs, his body wasn't as defined. But now, as he pulls his hair back, tying it up into a knot, I can't help but take in the way his biceps and shoulders ripple as he lifts and lowers his arms. The way his abs somehow get even tighter when he reaches for his jeans and unbuttons and unzips them. My eyes stay trained on him as he pushes his jeans and boxers down his muscular thighs, and my jaw damn near drops when his thick, veiny cock springs up, and the glint of metal catches my attention.

Oh, God… that piercing, the one that goes through the head of his dick from top to bottom—I looked it up once out of curiosity, and it's called an apadravya. And even though I was hurt by what he did when he pushed me away, that piercing has appeared in my thoughts and fantasies on several occasions when I was alone and needing a visual to get myself off.

Gage steps out of his clothes and reaches for his cock, stroking it up and down slowly, teasingly, as he smirks knowingly at me. I *might've* mentioned to the other women during our playdate how hot Gage's pierced cock was. And Kendall and Layla *might've* said something to their husbands about wanting them to get theirs pierced. And Gage *might've* found out... But in my defense, Kendall gave me wine and practically dragged it out of me.

Wanting Gage's pierced cock in me ASAP, I reach up to remove my own shirt, but he shakes his head, then stalks forward, crawling onto the bed and toward me like he's a lion, and I'm his prey. I get up on my knees and meet him halfway, and he lifts my sweater dress up, tossing it to the side.

"You're so damn perfect," he murmurs, dipping his head and trailing hot kisses across the swells of my breasts before he reaches behind me and unclasps my bra, removing each of the straps and setting my breasts free of their confines.

Taking them in his hands, he licks and sucks my nipples while I reach down and stroke his cock, using the bit of precum that's seeped out as lubricant.

"I want you in me," I groan when he sucks hard on my nipples, sending a jolt of electricity straight to my core.

"Soon, baby," he murmurs, leaning in and taking my bottom lip between his teeth. He tugs on it, then bites down before licking the bit of pain away.

Gently, Gage pushes me onto my back and peppers kisses along my flesh, stopping to lick my pebbled nipples, then works his way down my torso, pressing open-mouthed kisses to each of my hip bones. He stops at the top of my mound and kisses me through the material before removing my panties and dropping them onto the floor.

With my legs spread for him, he disappears from my line of sight and devours my pussy, licking my clit and working me toward an orgasm. Just as I'm about to come, he thrusts a finger and then two into me, curving them up and pushing me straight off the ledge.

Only once my legs have stopped shaking and my body has come down slightly does he stop and look up at me with a satisfied smirk on his face. "I could eat you every damn day," he says, making a show of licking my juices off his lips.

"I wouldn't protest." I shrug, lifting onto one elbow and wrapping my hand around his neck to draw him closer. "But right now, I really need you inside me."

Our mouths connect at the same time as Gage enters me, his tongue sliding past my parted lips as I release a moan, my body stretching in the best way to accommodate his thick erection.

Once he's all the way in, he stops and focuses on kissing me, tasting, coaxing, consuming me. And then he moves, his piercing rubbing my walls and eliciting pleasure. The last time we were together, it was about grieving and getting lost, escaping our heartbreak. But as Gage kisses me tenderly, his body moving in and out of me in a lazy rhythm, this is nothing like before. Gage isn't fucking me to forget. He's making love to me, showing me in every kiss and every slow thrust how much I mean to him.

Flashbacks of the night he pushed me away hit me hard, and I try to shake them out, but like my panic attack earlier, they have a mind of their own. Images of those women touching him, caressing him, pleasuring him. I take a deep breath, reminding myself that the Gage from back then isn't the same Gage who's in me, kissing me. This Gage... *my* Gage is clean and sober.

As if he can hear my thoughts and sense my insecurities, he breaks our kiss, his eyes meeting mine. "Stay with me, Sadie," he murmurs, brushing his soft yet strong lips across my own. "You're the only one for me. Stay right here with me, where we belong, in this moment, together."

"Gage," I whisper back against his lips. "Please don't hurt me."

His heated gaze sears into me. "The only thing I want to do is love you, baby."

As our mouths connect once again in a fiery-hot passionate kiss and our bodies come together in the most intimate way, I know that letting Gage in is worth the risk of getting hurt. Because for the first time since my world came crashing down on me almost two years ago, I feel like I'm finally living again... because of Gage. Because through the darkness of our despair and grief, we created our own light: Rory. And through her, as if it were fate, we've found our way back to each other. And while whatever we're doing might end in heartbreak, I'm going to do as Gage asked and live in the moment with him. Let him love me and spend every day loving him. Because really, isn't that all we have—right now, at this moment?

"I CAME IN YOU," GAGE MURMURS AS HE SPOONS ME FROM BEHIND, PEPPERING KISSES along my neck and shoulder. After we both found our release, instead of cleaning up, he rolled us over and demanded to hold me for a little while. And since I wasn't ready for the moment to end, I didn't argue.

"I'm on birth control, so we're good." Although the point of protection is also to protect us from STDs, and we haven't had that talk yet.

Once again, it's as if he can read my mind because he turns me over to face him and says, "I'm clean. I haven't been with anyone since you."

I flinch at his words since they're not entirely true. "You were with those women after me," I say, hating to ruin the mood but feeling the need to say it.

"Maybe." He sighs. "But I don't remember that night at all. I passed out and couldn't tell you what happened. I know I must've been with them in some way for you to walk out the door, and I saw them when Declan woke me up, but you're the last person I remember being with. I was tested for everything because of the drugs and the possibility of what I'd done, and I'm clean." He pulls me into his arms and nestles his face in the curtain of my hair. "I would do anything to take the hurt away that I caused you, but the truth is, without you walking out the door, I never would've gotten the help I needed. It was you…" He pulls back and looks into my eyes. "It was you coming into my life and making me feel, and then walking away and making me miss you, that led to me hitting rock bottom and getting help."

I nod in understanding. "I didn't see you have sex with those women. One was going down on you, and the other was all over you, but you weren't really participating. Maybe you didn't have sex with them. Maybe you did. We'll never know. All that matters is that we're both here now. You're clean and sober, and we're living for the moment. I won't punish you for your past because it's not fair to you, but I will tell you right now, like the papers we signed for Rory, that if you use, we're gone. The same goes for if you cheat on me. I won't tolerate it."

"That'll never happen," Gage says, his voice strong and determined. "I meant what I said, Sadie. You're the only one for me. I want your present, but I also want your future." He kisses me softly, tenderly, making me sigh into his touch. "And I'm going to spend every day showing you that until you fully understand and believe it."

"BABY, WAKE UP," GAGE MURMURS INTO MY EAR.

I crack a lid open and see it's still dark outside, then listen for Rory. When I don't hear her, telling me she's still asleep, I shake my head and roll away from him, wanting to sleep a little longer. When you're a mom, you never take sleep for granted, and when you spend all night getting fucked by a man like Gage, well, you need every minute of rest you can get.

"Rory's awake, baby, and the Easter Bunny came."

"What?" I ask, rolling back over and looking up at him. "What are you talking—?"

As if on cue, Rory shrieks from her room, "Ow, ow!" demanding to be let out of her crib.

She goes quiet, and then a loud bang rings out, making Gage and me go running. When we arrive at her room, we find her toddling toward the door, a huge grin lighting up her face.

"Holy shit," Gage breathes, lifting her into his arms. "She just pulled a damn Spider-Man and climbed her ass out."

"Ow, ow!" She giggles as Gage blows raspberries into her neck and settles her on the changing table to change her diaper.

"The crib is at the lowest point. Looks like it's time for a big girl bed." I give Rory a kiss on her forehead.

"Big girl bed?"

"Yep, a toddler bed. It's low to the ground so she won't fall out like in the crib. Collin moved into one just after his first birthday," I say, remembering the day we surprised him with his race car bed. It was just before Vincent got promoted at work, before he started working too many hours, despite his dad telling him he didn't have anything to prove. Before the pills came into play and turned my husband into a stranger. Picking out the bed was one of the last memories I have of him being sober and of us as a happy family.

"Well, it looks like Princess Rory will be getting a big girl bed for her birthday," Gage says, bringing me back to the present. "Everything's closed today for Easter, but we can go shopping tomorrow." He leans over and gives Rory a kiss on her cheek, then sets her on the floor.

"Where'd you get that dress?" I ask, watching as Rory toddles out of the room in a cute multicolored pastel dress with tiny Easter eggs all over the tutu.

"The Easter Bunny brought it." Gage shrugs.

"Oh, yeah?" I say with a laugh, remembering he said the Easter Bunny came when he was trying to wake me up. "What else did he bring?"

"Mama!" Rory shrieks.

"Better go find out." Gage winks, taking off after Rory.

The living room is filled with pastel-colored balloons, and on the coffee table, right at Rory's level, is a massive Easter basket, filled to the brim with toys and stuffed animals.

After taking a picture of Rory with the basket, Gage sets it on the floor, and Rory attacks it, finding a large stuffed bunny and bringing it to her chest to hug and kiss it.

As I watch Gage and Rory tear through the basket, memories of Collin's excitement hit me hard, but instead of letting myself wallow, I allow myself to embrace the memory before I bring myself back to the moment and sit with Gage and Rory, choosing to live in the now.

"Thank you," I tell him, kissing his cheek after we lay Rory down for her morning nap. After she wakes up, we'll head to Declan and Kendall's for an Easter barbecue.

"For what?" Gage pulls me into his arms and sits on the couch with me on his lap.

"For playing Easter Bunny when I couldn't."

He quirks a brow, so I explain, wanting him to know what's going through my head. A part of letting him in means talking to him, even when it's hard. "When we were visiting the Easter Bunny, I wasn't completely honest. I said that when Rory got older, she would get a basket, but the truth is, when Collin was Rory's age, we celebrated the holidays. I would dress him up and take pictures for Christmas, Easter, and even Valentine's Day. We would go see Santa and the Easter Bunny, and even though he wasn't even a year old yet, there were presents under the tree from Santa and a basket from the bunny.

"But after he died, I stopped celebrating, and when Rory was born, I was so afraid to move on without Collin, to create new memories without my baby boy, that I kept telling myself Rory was too young, and I'd do it once she was older. But it wasn't her age. It was my guilt that was stopping me." Tears fill my eyes, and Gage immediately wipes them away.

"She deserves to have these moments, even if she won't remember them, and I should've given them to her."

Gage frames my face in his hands. "Everyone grieves in their own way, and that little girl is so damn loved by you. Maybe you weren't ready to have her sit on some creepy people's laps yet, and you didn't buy her a basket, but she's loved every day."

"They're not creepy!" I laugh through my tears. "They're magical."

Twenty-Four

Gage

"I SAW THE PICTURES OF COLLIN SITTING ON SANTA'S LAP, NEXT TO HIS EASTER BASKET, when he was clearly younger than Rory. Dressed for the Fourth of July, his first birthday pictures. When Sadie was unpacking, she had a box of his stuff, and she left it open, and I looked. I saw. So when she told me Rory was too young and then had the panic attack, I called you, wanting your take on it," I tell Viola with Sadie sitting next to me.

We're at my therapist appointment together. Viola wanted to start small, get to know Sadie a bit, so she's talked about moving to New York, being an editor, and how we picked out a toddler bed for Rory yesterday—pink with a girly canopy that Rory loved.

When she asked how our Easter was, it led to Sadie telling her how hard it was for her. Yet she felt like she wasn't alone anymore because she had me, and that when she dropped the ball, I picked it up. So I felt it was only fair that I was completely honest with her.

"I knew there was a chance I was wrong," I continue, "and that it was just a coincidence, but something in me had me follow my gut, so I went out to the twenty-four-hour Walmart while Sadie and Rory were asleep."

Taking Sadie's hand in mine, I bring it up to my lips for a kiss. "When I saw the look on your face," I say, directing my words at Sadie instead of Viola. "As you watched Rory excitedly tear through the basket, snapping picture after picture, I had a feeling I was right. I wasn't going to ask, though. I didn't want to upset you. So when you brought it up and thanked me... letting me in... it meant the world to me."

Sadie sniffles. "Sometimes I want to talk to you, but I can't. Not that you won't listen, but it just doesn't come out. Like the words are stuck in my throat. Memories surface, and I feel like I'm being choked by the emotion."

Viola smiles softly at Sadie. "That's completely normal. This week, I'd like for you guys to try something."

I groan playfully, already knowing what's coming. "This is when she gives us homework," I tell Sadie. "Viola loves to give homework. It's not like the homework we had in school, though. It's worse. Because it makes you actually think and feel, and unlike in school, you can't fucking cheat."

Viola laughs. "Your homework is to buy a notebook and keep it on the counter until one of you needs it. When you feel like you can't speak," she says to Sadie. "Or you want to express how you feel." She looks at me. "I want you to write in it and give it to the other person. Communicating doesn't always have to be speaking. Gage writes songs, and you edit novels. Writing can be communicating too."

After thanking Viola—and Sadie agreeing to join me again next time—we head out. Since Kaylee and Braxton are spending the afternoon and evening with Rory, we use the alone time to pick up gifts for her upcoming birthday and order a cake. We've decided to do her birthday at A Latte Fun, renting the place out for the afternoon since Rory loves it there.

"Where are we going?" Sadie asks when Paul drives toward her condo instead of Kaylee and Braxton's place.

"I'm taking you out on a date."

Her eyes widen, and then a bright smile spreads across her face. "Really? Where? What about Rory?"

"We'll pick her up after dinner."

"I can't even remember the last time I ate at an adult restaurant without Rory." Sadie laughs.

We go by the condo, where a dress and heels wait for Sadie, thanks to Kendall, who had them sent over in her size from some trendy boutique she loves. While Sadie gets changed, doing her hair and makeup, I change into a suit since the place we're going to has a dress code.

When she steps out, donning a tight-fitted, off-the-shoulder emerald dress that matches her eyes and shows off every perfect curve she has, I reconsider going out, so I can eat her for dinner instead.

"The only reason I'm not canceling dinner and laying you out on this table is because you're too beautiful not to show off." I kiss her hard, my tongue delving past her parted lips so I can have a taste of her before I reluctantly pull back.

"You look sexy in a suit," she says, running her hands along the sleeves of my jacket. "I want to go to dinner, but maybe if we eat quickly, you can lay me out on the table for dessert."

With a chaste kiss on the corner of my mouth, she saunters away from me in her fuck me heels, leaving me determined to make dinner a quick affair.

Paul picks us up and drives us to Plush, a restaurant owned by Brody Fields, a friend of Braxton's. When I asked him where I should take Sadie since I've been out of the game for... well, ever, he said he'd take care of it for me. As we're led back to our private room, I make a mental note to buy Braxton that guitar he was talking about at practice the other day to thank him for hooking me up.

The hostess seats us, and I sit on the same side as Sadie, wanting to be close to her during dinner because there's no way I'm going an entire meal with her looking like she does and not touching her. After ordering our drinks and food, the server returns with Sadie's white wine and my water and lets us know our dinner will be ready soon.

Since the room has a private balcony, when the server leaves, I take Sadie's hand in mine and walk us over to it.

"Dance with me?" I ask, pressing the button on the wall that adjusts the volume. Sadie nods and steps into my arms, encircling her hands around my neck while mine wrap around her waist. Her head rests against my chest, and as we sway to the music, I can't help but feel like I'm right where I was meant to be. I have a healthy, amazing daughter, a beautiful girlfriend, and I'm living my life instead of barely surviving. After I lost Tori, I never imagined this for my life and didn't think I deserved it. Maybe in a lot of ways I don't, but fuck if I'm not going to hold on to it with everything in my being.

"Do you think anyone would know if I dropped to my knees right now and sucked your dick?" Sadie asks, shocking the hell out of me and making me laugh. I'm over here lost in my emotions, and she's thinking about my damn cock.

Jesus, can she get any more perfect?

Without waiting for an answer, she backs up and closes the French doors that lead to the private room where we're supposed to be eating dinner, then smirks like a goddamn little minx before she drops to her knees. At the same time, I stand frozen in place, wondering if she's really about to suck me off right here on the private balcony in Plush.

She answers my thoughts when she unbuttons and unzips my pants, then pulls my cock out. Wrapping my semi-hard shaft in her hand, she presses a soft kiss to the head, looking up at me through her lashes. With her eyes never leaving mine, she darts her tongue out, licking the metal piercing, then sucks gently on it. She parts her lips and takes me all the way down her damn throat, not stopping until I'm bottoming out in the back.

"Holy shit," I breathe, grabbing the railing with one hand for support and her head with my other to… fuck, I don't even know what I'm grabbing her head for. All I know is that her hot, wet mouth wrapped around my cock is the sexiest thing I've ever seen and felt, and if I don't slow her down, I'm going to explode in less than thirty seconds like a pubescent fucking boy.

But before I can say or do anything, she takes me all the way into her throat again, hollowing her cheeks and sucking me down like she doesn't have a damn gag reflex, and I'm done for. I come down her throat, watching as she takes it all, swallowing every drop until I'm completely drained. And when there's nothing left, she slowly pulls her mouth off my shaft, stopping at the head to kiss it.

I pull her into my arms and crash my mouth down on hers, not giving a shit that the taste of her is tinged with the salt from my cum. Spinning her around, I back her against the stone wall and shove my hand between her legs, groaning into her mouth when my fingers land on her soaked-through panties.

Pushing them aside, I thrust two fingers into her, my thumb finding her swollen clit. I finger-fuck her like I'm kissing her, slow and deep. She detonates around my fingers a few short seconds later, soaking my hand. And when her legs nearly give out on her, I grip the curve of her hip to hold her up as she comes completely undone.

We stay like this for several moments, both of us catching our breaths. Once we're somewhat composed, we head back inside the private room, finding our food waiting for us.

"When I was growing up, my mom said I wasn't allowed to have any snacks before dinner because it would ruin my appetite." Sadie smirks. "She was totally wrong because I'm still hungry... for dinner and more of you."

Fuck, have I mentioned how damn perfect my woman is?

"DADA, DADA!" RORY GIGGLES, DROPPING HER LITTLE BUTT ONTO THE IN-GROUND trampoline so I can jump and make her fly. When I do what she wants, and she flies into the air, I catch her in my arms, making her laugh harder.

It's the day of her birthday party, which is also her actual birthday. It's crazy to think my princess is already one. I've only known her—known about her—for two months, but it feels like she's a part of me. I can't imagine her or Sadie not being a part of my life. I'm not technically living with them, but I'm there every night, and I haven't once not slept next to Sadie since the night she asked me to stay. I'm working on finding us a home, and once I find the perfect place, my plan is to propose and ask her to move in together. I never had a home growing up, and while the condo is great, I want to give Rory what I always dreamed of: the big house and even bigger backyard with a jungle gym and a dog running around.

"You must be Gage," a woman says, making me glance up from my daughter. I instantly recognize her as the woman from the cemetery.

"Ga ga!" Rory exclaims, reaching for her.

"Hello, sweetheart," the woman says to Rory before turning her attention back to me. "I'm Janice, and my husband, Henry, is saying hello to Sadie. We're… Vincent's parents." Her eyes dim at the mention of his name.

"It's nice to meet you." Sadie's mentioned them a few times since we've been together, telling me they've stayed in touch and consider Rory like a granddaughter. I didn't put the two together until now, though. That the couple from the cemetery are Sadie's in-laws.

"I just wanted to say thank you," she says softly. "Sadie has told us so much about you, and it's clear you make her happy. Vincent might've been my son, but I wasn't oblivious to the way he treated her and chose drugs over her."

Her admission has me swallowing thickly because I also chose drugs over Sadie once upon a time. As if she can sense my thoughts, she adds, "He refused to get help, and instead of doing what we should've done and cut him off, we enabled him. Sadie said you've been clean for over a year now. That's all I wanted for my son…" She runs her fingers through Rory's hair. "Seeing Sadie so happy makes me happy, and I know I have you to thank for that."

"She and Rory are my world," I tell her honestly. "Their happiness is everything to me, and I'll always do everything in my power to make sure they're happy." I hand Rory over to Janice, making it clear that includes having no issue with her and her husband being part of our lives.

"Hey, you," Sadie says shyly, stepping over and kissing my cheek. "I see you've met Janice."

"I have," I say, tucking her under my arm. "Things are about to get crazy since we finished our album and will start promoting it, but we should get together for dinner when it calms down." I don't miss the way Sadie sighs in relief against my side.

"That would be great," Janice says, kissing Rory and setting her down so she can run and play with the other kids she's made friends with.

She walks over to her husband, who's chatting with Easton, and Sadie wraps her arms around me tightly, looking up at me. "Thank you."

"You don't have to thank me for accepting your family. Vincent and I both fucked up. The only difference between us is that I was able to get help before I killed myself. I know how fortunate I am to have this second chance with you and be able to have Rory in my life." I lean down and kiss her soft lips. "I could've easily been in the same position as him, and I'll never, for a second, forget that."

"Mama! Dada!" Rory yells, wanting our attention.

"Let's go sing 'Happy Birthday' to our princess," I murmur to Sadie. "Then figure out a way to make her stop growing."

Twenty-Five
Gage

"I'M SENDING YOU GUYS A SCHEDULE FOR THE UPCOMING PROMO AND ENGAGEMENTS you'll be required to attend," Mario, our publicist, says, glancing up from his phone. We've finalized the album, titled *Calm After the Storm*, and are going over all the shit that comes next. "But I wanted to let you know that tonight you'll be performing at Ruckus. I know it's last minute, but the artist who was supposed to perform got sick." The name of the club sends a shiver down my spine. It's been over a year since I've been in a club, and Ruckus is one of the crazier ones. I spent too much time in VIP, getting high after our performances.

"Tonight?" Camden groans. "Tomorrow's Mother's Day."

"Layla will be working as well," Mario says. "Since you guys are making a comeback, we'll document everything into a vlog series. It's all in the informational packet I emailed."

"She approved that?" Camden asks, pulling out his phone to call his wife, who's one of Blackwood's videographers and has been mostly on leave since she gave birth to Marianna—aside from doing a few small gigs like Kendall and Declan's music video.

"I did," she says, walking in, all business. "I actually just got out of a meeting a few minutes ago, or I would've told you. You know I've been thinking about going back to work, and your dad agreed to me coming back part-time, working with you guys on the promo for your upcoming album."

Camden grins, no doubt loving that he'll have his wife around. One of the things that sucks about putting out an album is how busy we get with promo. I'm already dreading all the time I'll be away from Sadie and Rory, but it's all part of the game, and once it's done, we'll take some time off before we go on tour. I'm hoping to convince her to join us, at least some of the time, so I don't have to go too long without seeing my girls.

"Anything else?" Braxton asks, standing and ready for this meeting to be over.

Mario looks over his notes. "Nope. Be at Ruckus tonight at eight o'clock for the sound check."

We all take off, and I head home, only stopping at the deli to pick us up dinner. Since Paul is driving, I allow myself to get lost in my thoughts. I'd be lying if I said I wasn't nervous about tonight. It's the first time I'll be back in the environment that enabled me to drown myself in my sorrows and grief. Somehow, it feels like I'm being given a test that I still don't feel prepared for even though I've studied. I pull out my phone, texting Kaylee to see if she's going. She immediately responds that she was planning to, but if I want Sadie to go and need a sitter, she'd be more than happy to watch Rory. I thank her and tell her that I'll let her know, and then I text my therapist, asking if she's available. When she hasn't responded by the time I get home, I put my phone away to focus on my girls.

When I walk in the door, Rory is crying, and Sadie is cradling her in her arms. It's not often Rory cries. I don't have any babies to compare her to, but she seems extremely chill. Unless she's teething, she sleeps all night and rarely throws tantrums.

"What happened?" I ask, dropping the food onto the table and walking over to them.

"I was trying to get some editing done, and she got into the cabinets... slammed her finger in the door."

"Is she okay? Do we need to take her to the hospital?"

"She's okay." Sadie sighs. "It just hurt and scared her. She refused to take a nap today, and I'm running behind on a manuscript that's due. I usually work while she naps or sleeps, but I've been a little preoccupied lately." She glances at me, her cheeks staining pink, and I smirk, remembering the way I took her last night in the shower after we put Rory to bed and then again in bed while we were watching TV. I can't get enough of her, and the moment Rory is asleep, I spend our time together all over her. I hadn't thought about the fact that means she isn't getting her work done, but she hasn't once complained or said anything.

"Do you want me to take her so you can get some work done?" I ask, reaching out for Rory, who's calmed slightly, and taking her into my arms.

"No, it's okay. But I need to get this done tonight, so maybe..." She twists her lips, and my stomach drops at the thought of her not wanting me to spend the night.

"I actually have a thing tonight," I say, knowing her going is out of the question. There's no way I can ask her to attend a show when she needs to get her own work done.

"Oh, okay," she says, her lips turning down into a slight frown.

"It's a work thing," I explain as Rory lays her head on my shoulder and cuddles into my front. "I was going to ask you to come. It's at Ruckus."

"The club?" She sounds as worried as I feel. I don't want to weigh her down with my shit since she's stressed enough as it is, so I force a smile and shrug like it's not a big deal.

"Yeah, we're performing our new single there. It'll be videoed and put on YouTube to help generate a buzz around the upcoming album. It gets fans hyped. We don't do it often anymore, but since we've been gone for a while, it'll help put our name back on the board."

"Makes sense," she says. "Looks like Rory finally fell asleep." She nods toward our sleeping little girl. "Hopefully that doesn't mean she'll wake up in the middle of the night." She rolls her eyes.

"Should I wake her up?" I ask, unsure what to do. Every day I learn something new about parenting.

"No, just lay her down, so we can eat in peace." She waves me off. "How long until you have to leave?"

I glance at the clock. "I need to get ready and head out in about an hour."

"What songs are you guys playing?" Sadie asks as we eat, making small talk while she also messages back and forth with one of her clients, who's asking her questions about a manuscript she sent her.

"A mixture of our new songs and some old," I say, trying not to freak out over having to enter that club. Every time my brain goes to the music, the people, the drugs, I feel like I want to throw up. I knew this day would eventually come, and I thought I was ready, but now I'm second-guessing myself.

"Hopefully, it's just three songs, and then we're out," I mutter, pushing my food away. The last thing I need is to throw up on stage.

"Yeah," she says, her attention on her texts. I watch her for a few minutes, hating how stressed she looks. I mentioned she doesn't need to work, that I can provide for us, but she just gave me a crazy look and said she appreciated it, but this is the twenty-first century, and she's an independent woman. I think it was meant mostly as a joke, but deep down, I'm sure a part of her doesn't want to depend on another addict—even if I am a recovering one.

Sadie glances up from her phone, catching me staring, and quirks a brow. "You okay?"

I want to tell her I'm nowhere near close to okay, that I'm freaking out on the inside, wondering what the hell I'm thinking going into a club so soon, but when her phone goes off again and she groans in frustration at whoever she's conversing with, I simply nod.

After dinner, Sadie says she's going back to work while I jump in the shower and get ready for tonight. With my nerves making me anxious, I take an extra-long time in the shower, trying to rid myself of the anxiety weighing on me.

After kissing Rory—who's still asleep—and Sadie goodbye, I head out to meet the guys at the club. Since it's one of those events where we need to be seen, we drive together, and our security follows us in. Even with the late notice, the area is filled with screaming fans as we walk up the black carpet that leads to the club. With a lump in my throat the size of a golf ball, I try to act as chill as possible. My phone goes off in my pocket, and when I look to see if it's Sadie, I find a text from Viola: **Hey Gage, I was tied up. I can talk now if you want to call me.**

I want to tell her I can hide in the fucking bathroom to talk to my therapist, but the band needs me, so instead, I shoot her a text that it's all good and I'll see her at our next appointment. Then I pocket my phone, willing myself to summon up the strength I need to get through tonight.

Twenty-Six

Sadie

I'M NECK-DEEP IN EDITS WHEN A TEXT PINGS ON MY PHONE. I GLANCE AT IT AND SEE IT'S Kaylee, asking where I am.

> **Me:** At home…

> **Kaylee:** Oh! I thought you were at Ruckus. I told Gage I could watch Rory for you if you needed a sitter. I just got here. The guys sound so good. Braxton was worried about Gage since he hasn't played for an audience since he's been back, but he seems to be doing good. Did he seem nervous before he left?

Her text is accompanied by a short video of the guys on stage, playing a single I've heard them rehearsing in the studio, "Hurricane." Kaylee zooms in on each of the guys, all of them clearly in their element until she gets to Gage. He's playing, nodding his head in the way he does when he's focused, but something about his eyes has me pressing pause. He looks distant, disconnected, like he's just trying to get through the motions. Her question has me thinking about earlier tonight. I was so caught up in the chaos of my job that I was only half there while we were eating dinner.

Did he seem nervous? I can't remember…But regardless, even if he didn't appear to be, tonight is a big deal, and I'm not there to support him.

And then I remember what he said when he first got home. *I was going to ask you to go…*I was so distracted that my only focus was getting time alone to finish my edits.

Dammit, I should be there, supporting him.

Pulling up my contacts, I call Janice. It's late, but she and Henry have always been night owls. "Hey, sweetie, is everything okay?"

"Yes…no. Gage is at his first show since…" I swallow thickly, realizing by the second how badly I've messed up. One of the main reasons he was scared to record again was because of everything that comes with being in a rock band. He mentioned on several occasions that he was afraid the music would always be associated with his addiction, and he worried he wouldn't be able to separate the two. "Is there any way you could come over and watch Rory? I know it's late and at the last minute, but—"

"Henry and I will be right over," Janice says.

"Thank you."

While I wait for them to arrive, I get dressed in my most "club-appropriate" attire, thankful it actually fits since it's from pre-kids. When Henry and Janice get here, I call for an Uber and arrive at the club a little over an hour after Kaylee texted me. There's a chance the band isn't even playing anymore, but since I haven't heard from Gage, I figure it can't hurt to go in and see if I can catch him still playing. Since my name isn't on the list, I text Kaylee, who meets me at the door. The second our eyes lock, I know something's wrong.

"The guys can't find him," she says. "Security is looking for him right now. They finished playing, and part of the contract is that they hang out and have a drink. One minute, Gage was there, and the next, he wasn't."

I rush past her, my heart pounding, needing to find Gage. I can feel it deep inside me as if a string connects us that something is wrong. The club is packed, and there's no way I'm going to find him in this chaos, so I pull my phone out and dial his number. It rings several times before he answers. "Sadie," he whispers, his voice sounding broken.

"Gage, where are you?"

"I...I'm having..."

"Baby, just tell me where you are. I'm here, at Ruckus."

"Bathroom."

I hang up and search for the bathroom. After asking someone, I find it and push past the guys standing outside, waiting for their turn. The door is locked, so I get a manager to let me in. At first, he's unsure, but when I explain who I am and who's in there, he reluctantly does as I ask.

Shutting and locking the door behind me, I find Gage sitting in the corner, his face in his hands, and his body visibly shaking.

"Gage."

His head shoots up, his glassy eyes meeting mine, and I cut across the room and into his lap. "Oh, Gage." I frame his face with my hands. "Did you...did you take anything?" I hate to ask, but I need to know where to go from here.

"No." He shakes his head. "It just...it was too much." He drops his head against my chest and releases a guttural sob. "I was okay playing, but then we were supposed to stay, and I should've left. The guys said I could leave, but I didn't want to let them down and have people talking shit that I dipped out early, so I stayed."

I hold him tight while he cries, peppering kisses all over his face, needing him to know I'm here. When he finally calms, he takes a deep breath and looks into my eyes. "You came."

"I'll always be here. We're a team. You just have to tell me you need me, and I'll be here. Always. Just like when I had a panic attack, and you carried me to safety, or when I was drowning in my grief and couldn't give Rory the Easter she deserved. You were there for me, and I'll always be here for you." I kiss him softly on his lips, then stand, so he can get up as well.

Gage threads his fingers through mine, and we walk out of the bathroom together, ignoring the looks he's getting. Hopefully tomorrow people will just assume we were having sex in the bathroom.

Wanting to get out of there as quickly as possible, Gage texts the guys to let them know that he left, and he'll talk to them tomorrow, and then we head out. Paul drives us home, and after thanking Janice and Henry for keeping an eye on Rory, we shower and change into comfortable clothes.

"I need to call my sponsor," Gage says once we're cuddled on the couch. "I'd like for you to meet him."

"I'd be honored."

"Gage, how are you?" Gabe says, wiping his eyes and clicking a light on.

"I'm...all right...now." He turns the phone so I'm in view. "This is Sadie, my girlfriend and Rory's mom."

Gabe smiles. "Nice to meet you."

"You, too."

"I had a show tonight," Gage admits softly, so unlike the rock star persona other people see. "I wasn't going to use, but it brought back a shit ton of memories and scared the hell out of me. I didn't like feeling like that."

Gabe nods. "What did you do?"

"Went to the bathroom and hid like a little bitch."

"Hey!" I say, glaring at him. "Don't you ever say that again. You didn't hide anywhere. You got out of the situation the best way you could. This was your first time being at a club. Of course, it's going to trigger you. You're human. You could've easily allowed yourself to drown in the feeling and used, but instead, you handled it. And that's more than what many recovering addicts would do," I say, trying not to compare Gage to my late husband, but I can't help it. Looking at Gage, seeing how hard this is for him, but also seeing how strong he is without even realizing it, makes me so proud of him. "You did the right thing, Gage. You got yourself out of the situation."

"She's right," Gabe says, making me jump. I completely forgot he was on the phone. "It could've ended much differently."

"I froze," Gage says. "I should've called you. I didn't call anyone. I just sat in the bathroom and freaked out."

"But did you use?" Gabe asks.

"No," Gage breathes. "Never again." The conviction in his voice sends shivers down my spine.

The guys talk for a few more minutes, and Gage mentions he's going to attend a meeting tomorrow and call Viola for an emergency appointment, and then they hang up.

"I'm so proud of you," I tell Gage, climbing into his lap.

"What if this is a sign that I can't have the career I used to have? What does this mean for the band?"

"Of course, you can have it. You just have to take it one day at a time and adjust accordingly. You said it yourself, you should've left, but you stayed when we both know your friends, your *family*, would never have wanted you to stay if they knew how you felt. You can have the music without the lifestyle, and the guys will understand. Hell, they're all married. They're just trying to make music and entertain the fans themselves."

253

I wrap my arms around his neck and look into his blue eyes. "Let people in, Gage. Let me in. We love you and support you."

Gage stills under me, and I realize what I've just said. I could play it off, but there's no point since I meant it. "I love you, Gage. And I want to be here, by your side, and the person you call when you're feeling alone. Tonight, you should've told me how you felt. In the future, talk to me."

"Fuck," Gage mutters, crashing his mouth down on mine. He kisses me hard and rough as if he's trying to convey every emotion he feels in that one kiss. When we break apart, he rests his forehead against mine. "I love you so much, Sadie."

Twenty-Seven

Gage

"DADA!" RORY SQUEALS, WAKING ME UP. I ROLL OVER AND FIND SADIE STILL ASLEEP. After getting home and talking to my sponsor, I spent the next couple of hours getting lost in her. I showed her how much she means to me and how much I love and need her. We didn't fall asleep until the sun was damn near coming up, so she had to be exhausted.

Carefully, so she doesn't wake up, I grab Rory and change her diaper and get her dressed. It's Mother's Day, and even though I already bought Sadie a gift, I want to do more to show her how much she means to Rory and me. I consider calling Paul to pick us up, but since it's a nice day out, I write Sadie a note, letting her know I took Rory with me in her stroller—so she doesn't freak out—and then we take off on our mission to spoil Sadie.

On the way to the store, I pick up some flowers and make a pit stop at Eternal Cross Cemetery. After placing the flowers on Tori's tombstone, I push Rory over to where her brother is.

"This is Collin," I tell her, taking her out and setting her on my lap. "He's your big brother." I know she doesn't understand, but Sadie wants her to know about him, and I completely support that. "Collin, this is your little sister, Aurora. We call her Rory." Rory squeals at the mention of her name, and I kiss her cheek.

Glancing between Collin's and Vincent's graves, I speak to them, hoping if there's a God, and they're in heaven, they can hear me. "I just wanted to let you know that I'm going to take care of Sadie. I love her, and like you, I want her to be happy." I turn my attention to Vincent's grave. "The only difference between you and me is that I survived. But I promise I'm going to live every day loving and taking care of Sadie, showing her how special she is."

I look at Collin's. "I'd give your mom up in a heartbeat if it meant you were here with her, but since it's not possible, I promise to make sure your spirit lives on. Your mom thinks about you every day, and even though you're not physically with us, you'll always be the best part of her."

I set flowers out for both of them and then lay the last bushel on the grave where Sadie's daughter was laid to rest. So much heartbreak in one place... Sadie deserves for her heart to be filled with love and happiness.

"All right, princess. We're going to pick up breakfast and then head home to Mommy."

"Pa pa!" she shrieks, pointing at the small park.

"Fine, but only for a few minutes."

When the stroller turns in the direction of the park, she yells in excitement. We spend the next half hour playing in the park, and luckily, when I say it's time to go, she doesn't freak out on me.

On the way home, we stop at the bakery and pick Sadie up breakfast and pastries, then stop at the store to get balloons. Her gift is already at the house.

"Boon!" Rory squeals, pointing at the balloons when they fly through the air as we walk back to the house. When we arrive, Sadie is lying across the couch, still in her pajamas, and reading on her tablet.

"Happy Mother's Day," I say, leaning over and giving her an upside-down kiss.

"Boon, Mama, boon!" Rory yells, making Sadie laugh.

"Thank you," she says, sitting up. "Did you have fun?" she asks Rory.

"We made a pit stop at the park." I set the food out and hand her a coffee. "We also stopped by Eternal Cross." Sadie nods in understanding, even if she doesn't completely understand.

I set Rory in her highchair and put some eggs and pieces of a biscuit on the plate for her, along with her sippy cup filled with milk, while Sadie sips her coffee and watches.

"What?" I ask, wondering if I'm doing something wrong.

"I trust you, Gage," she says, shocking the hell out of me. "I trust you with our daughter, and in the future, if you want to drive with her, I trust you to keep her safe."

Knowing that she wouldn't say that lightly, I pull her into my arms and kiss her. "Thank you. That means the world to me."

After we eat breakfast, Sadie opens her gifts. I got her a necklace with a Mom charm on it—hanging from it are her three babies' birthstones. She has me put it on her and tears up, thanking me. The next gift is from Rory. The other day Sadie had to run out to the store, so I stayed with Rory, and we created a picture for Sadie, using her hands to make a heart. I wrote a poem underneath it, and Rory scribbled on it, adding her own touch.

"Gage," Sadie gasps. "This is perfect." It's already framed, so we can hang it up in the living room. "This has been the best Mother's Day ever. Thank you."

"I have one more gift for you," I tell her, handing her the

envelope. She opens it and in it is a certificate to a day spa. Unsure what she would want, I purchased everything they offer, just in case.

"I've never been to a spa," she admits sheepishly. "Thank you."

"When I was growing up, my mom used to say all she wanted was a day at the spa to relax. She never got that day at the spa, but I'm so happy I can give one to you. I want to make you happy," I tell her, taking her hands in mine. "Rory and I are beyond lucky to have you, and I want you to know every day how much you mean to us."

Sadie nods, her eyes turning watery. "We're lucky to have each other."

We spend the rest of the day together, and then go to dinner with everyone for Mother's Day, heading back to Easton and Sophia's place afterward for dessert.

"Can we talk about last night?" Camden asks when everyone is hanging out and bullshitting. Normally, I'd be pissed he's throwing my shit out there, but since everyone in the room is family, I get it. They blame themselves for not speaking up when I was spiraling.

"I want to be part of the band," I tell everyone, as Sadie takes my hand in hers to remind me that she's here and by my side. "But I don't want..." I shake my head. "I *can't* be part of that lifestyle. The clubs and after-parties. I know I've been clean for over a year, but I was addicted for over six years. I didn't want to do drugs last night, but I couldn't handle the situation. It was too much for me, and I had a panic attack. Sadie found me in the bathroom."

Easton clasps me on the shoulder. "That's the first damn time you've ever told us your feelings, son," he says. "Thank you." He steps around and sits in front of me. "The only requirement in your contract is to make music. If something is put on your schedule that isn't good for you, you tell me. Got it?" I nod. "I'll make sure it's taken care of, *always*. You come first. All of you do." He glances at Cam, Brax, and Dec. "We're a family, and the only thing that matters is that you're healthy and happy."

Sadie sniffles, cuddling into my side, and I tuck her under my arm, glancing down at her. "See," she whispers. "You're not alone."

"No," I say, looking around at the people who, despite not being blood, are my family in every way that matters. "I'm not."

"HOLY SHIT. YES, RIGHT THERE," SADIE MOANS AS I DEVOUR HER PUSSY WITH MY FINGERS and tongue. After putting Rory to bed, Sadie and I showered the day off. She said she needed a few minutes, so I got dressed and picked up, knowing she likes it when the house is clean before she goes to bed. I was just finishing the dishes when she called me into the room, where I found her spread eagle on the bed dressed in a tiny as fuck black lace bra and panty set.

Her body coils tightly, and then, with a flick of my tongue, she soars, coming hard. Needing to be in her, I flip her onto her belly—the way I know she likes—and pull her up onto all fours before I line myself up and thrust into her from behind.

"This...You and me... is perfect," I groan, pulling back and then pushing into her. My hand comes down on her ass, making a cracking sound as it connects with her flesh.

"Again," she moans, wiggling her ass like the damn minx she is.

I pull out, smack it again, then plow into her, hitting deep.

"Oh, God, yes, again."

I do as she asks, fucking her with deep, lazy thrusts, alternating between smacking her sexy ass and massaging it. When her pussy tightens around me, telling me she's close, I pull her up so that her back is flush with my front and massage her clit until she's screaming my name in pure ecstasy, taking me straight over the edge with her.

Once we've both gotten a handle on our breathing, I pull her into my arms, our bodies naturally tangling up in one another. We should probably clean up since I'm sure my cum is dripping out of her, but the thought of her being full of me, even if she is on birth control, is such a damn turn-on. One day, I'm going to put another baby in her, and this time, I'll be there to watch her belly grow and swell. There was a time when the thought would've sent me to drugs, but now, it reminds me why I need to stay clean.

"I want this," Sadie says, shaking me from my thoughts. "Every day." There's no way she could know what I'm thinking, but the fact that we're on the same page tells me just how perfect we are together.

"I do too." I kiss her on her lips.

"What I mean is…" She bites her bottom lip nervously. "I want you and me… here… every day."

"Baby, you've got me." I glide my hand down her side and squeeze her peach of an ass. I don't know why she's suddenly acting like this, but I'll gladly remind her every day that I'm not going anywhere, that she and Rory are it for me.

"No… Ugh," she groans in frustration. "I want you to move in with me," she blurts out, her eyes going wide. "If you want to," she adds softly.

Rolling her onto her back, I cage her in my arms as my heart pounds against my rib cage. She spreads her legs and wraps them around me, pushing my hard shaft back inside her. With my cum still inside her, I slip right in.

"One day, I'm going to put a ring on your finger," I murmur, pressing a kiss to the corner of her mouth. "Then I'm going to put another baby in your belly." I kiss the other corner. "But until then…" I place a kiss on her neck. "There's nothing I want more than to go to bed and wake up with you in my arms every day for the rest of our lives."

Twenty-Eight

Gage

"WHAT'S UP, LA?" CAMDEN YELLS OVER THE ROARING CROWD. "YOU MISS US?" THE deafening screams of the fans are enough to make even the cockiest musician's heart sing. We're playing at the Summer Music Festival: an annual festival that houses all types of bands on the beach in LA. It's been over two years since we've played here, and I have to admit it's nice to be back. It also helps that as I gear up to play, Sadie is standing on the side of the stage, smiling and waving at me.

When the band got the news that we'd be playing a short set—which lines up with our single that released yesterday—I talked to Sadie, and we decided to make it a little getaway. Three of the nannies who work for Kendall and Layla have come along, so Rory's safely tucked into bed at our house in Calabasas with the other kids.

"Damn, it feels good to be back," Camden adds, making everyone scream all over again. He talks to the crowd for a few minutes, then announces that we'll be playing some new songs and to let us know what they think.

My gaze goes to my woman, who's dressed in a tiny black dress and tall as hell boots that go almost to her knees, cheering us on, and my heart swells in my chest. For the first time in a long time, I feel good about playing. It's not realistic to think she can be at every show but having her here while I work through my shit helps. Knowing that when I'm done and walk off the stage, she'll be there waiting for me makes me feel like the luckiest fucking guy in the world.

The first song starts, and that one rolls into the next. Before I know it, Camden is announcing the final song for the night, "Bleeding Heart."

The second my sticks hit the drums and Camden starts belting out the lyrics, I'm instantly overcome by the words, succumbing to the feeling that I get every time I hear the song I wrote for Sadie...

Emerald eyes, soft smile, big heart
She's everything a man could ever want
Makes it bittersweet to know there's a chance
She'll never be mine
Someone like me doesn't deserve her time
But that doesn't stop me from wanting to take what's mine
From wanting her heart to be mine
Her body, her soul, all mine

It's crazy to think about where we were when I wrote the song and how much our relationship has developed. I know without a doubt she's the one for me, and I'm going to propose soon. Life is too damn short, and I want to make her my wife.

Throughout the entire song, our eyes stay locked on each other, the sexual tension building with each word Camden sings. Words don't need to be spoken, the lyrics speaking for themselves. And by the time the song ends, and Camden is saying good night to the crowd, thanking them for being amazing, I'm pushing off my seat, throwing my sticks toward the crowd, and taking off after my woman.

As I stalk toward her, the heat in her gaze tells me she wants me as much as I want her. And when I close the last bit of distance between us, lifting her by her ass into my arms, she squeals, encircling her legs around my waist.

"I need you," she breathes, her mouth connecting with mine. I find the closest empty room and slam the door behind us. Pushing her against the door, I reach between us and grab her thin panties, ripping them straight off her body. She shrieks in shock, then kisses me harder, devouring my mouth with hers. I thrust a couple of fingers into her to make sure she's good to go and find she's soaking fucking wet.

"This is going to be hard and quick," I warn, knowing full well that as turned on as I am, there's zero chance of me drawing it out.

"Yes," she hisses as I pull my cock out and thrust it into her. With her weight above me, I go deep, and she groans, no doubt in a mixture of pain and pleasure as she takes every inch of me.

"Oh, God," she moans, her head falling back and her eyes rolling toward the ceiling. "That damn piercing is going to be the death of me."

I chuckle, loving that it brings her pleasure. After Tori and before Sadie, I never gave a shit about a woman's pleasure. I only got it for the pain it brought me. But seeing the way she loves it makes me glad I got it.

"Sadie," I groan. "I need you to touch yourself, baby." I hate that she'll have to help get herself off, but there's no way I'll be able to do it for her in this position.

"I'm already there," she breathes, bouncing herself up and down on my dick like it was made specifically for her pleasure. A moment later, she explodes around me, her pussy choking my dick like a vise, siphoning every drop of cum from me.

As I stay where I am, keeping her pinned against the door, her juices drip down and coat my balls. Walking us over to the table, I pull out and set her down, spreading her legs so I can see her glistening pussy dripping with my cum. She stays quiet, but I can feel her eyes on me as I push my fingers into her.

"What are you doing?" she asks, her voice coming out breathy.

"I want to have another baby," I admit, making her body tighten around my fingers. "I want my cum to fill this tight pussy over and over again until we make a baby." I press my thumb against her clit as I finger her, the only sound coming from her slick pussy.

If I was worried my admission would turn her off, I would be dead wrong because Sadie's moans get louder with every word I speak. "I want you swollen with my baby. And I want every man who sees you to know that I was inside you and we created that together.

"Do you want that, baby? Do you want me to fuck a baby into you?"

My question sends her over the edge, and she comes, yelling, "Yes," as I finger-fuck her right through her orgasm.

When she opens her eyes, she looks a mixture of sated and exhausted, and I chuckle at how fucking adorable she is.

"Did you mean that?" she asks, nibbling on the corner of her lip.

"That I want you pregnant? Yeah, one hundred percent." I pull my fingers out of her and stick them into my mouth, sucking her juices off them. When she sees what I've done, her eyes hood over, her tongue darting out across the seam of her lips.

I push my fingers back into her, then withdraw them, lifting them to her lips to paint her pouty mouth with our essence. "Any time you want to stop taking your birth control, I'm good with that."

"Are you sure?" she breathes.

I lean in and press my mouth to hers, kissing her tenderly, and she kisses me back. "I want everything with you," I murmur against her lips. "Anything you'll give me, I'll take and cherish."

"You have me," she says, framing my face. "All of me."

"WHY IS IT WHENEVER I'M ON A DEADLINE, RORY DECIDES SHE'S TOO GOOD FOR NAPTIME?" Sadie groans, dropping her head onto the desk and dramatically banging it on the wood, making Rory giggle.

"Mama bang bang." Rory toddles over to the desk and smacks her hand on the desk, mimicking her movement. "Rory bang bang."

I snort out a laugh and lift Rory into my arms. "I don't have anything else to do today. Why don't I get Rory out of your hair so you can work, and we'll bring home dinner?"

Sadie's head pops up. "Have I told you how much I love you?"

I chuckle. "Every day." I lean over and kiss her, and Rory does the same, copying me. "What do you say, princess? Want to go play at the park?"

"Yay!" Rory shrieks, smacking the sides of my face with her tiny hands. "Pa Pa!"

After changing her diaper and getting her dressed, I grab the stroller and buckle her in, shoving the diaper bag in the undercarriage.

"Say bye to Mommy," I tell Rory, who waves to Sadie.

"Bye, baby. Love you." Sadie glances at me. "Both of you."

"Love you."

The walk to the park doesn't take long, and once we arrive, Rory takes off like a bat out of hell, ready to make the jungle gym her bitch. She stops at the swings first, and I spend the next twenty minutes pushing her while playing duck and tickle. She giggles the entire time, thinking it's hilarious every time I duck and then pop up and tickle her.

When she grows tired of the swing, she runs to the jungle gym, climbing up the four levels that lead to the slide. I follow to make sure she's safe, and then run to the other end so I can catch her when she slides down, lifting her into my arms and blowing raspberries on her belly when she hits the bottom.

The third time she climbs up the levels, I run to the end to meet her, only when I get there, she isn't sitting on the slide ready to slide down.

"Rory?" I yell, just as a loud shriek pierces my ears. The cry that comes after can only be described as gut-wrenching. I run back, unsure what the hell happened when I see my daughter lying on the ground, crying in agony.

I jump into action, ready to pick her up when I notice her arm is dangling at the elbow. Her eyes, filled with pain, meet mine, and I swallow down my emotion, needing to help her.

"I've called an ambulance," a woman says as I carefully pick my baby up and rock her gently in my arms. As we wait for the paramedics to arrive, a flashback hits me hard…

"Excuse me… Are you Gage Sharp?"

I glance up and find a nurse standing above me. Unable to move, I simply nod, and she sits next to me.

"I'm not supposed to say anything. Tori's parents didn't want it to be mentioned, but I've seen you here for hours, and I heard your friend mention you were her boyfriend."

Were… past tense… because Tori is dead. She hung herself, ending her life and leaving me to mourn her.

"There's something you should know. Tori was pregnant."

I snap my head toward her. "What?"

"She wasn't far along, only about twelve weeks, but when they did the autopsy, they confirmed it was a girl. I'm sorry," she says, gently placing her hand on my arm. "I just thought you might want to know."

The nurse sits next to me for several minutes while I sob into my hands, wondering why Tori would take her own life, knowing she was pregnant with my baby. She had to know I would take care of her. It doesn't make any sense. And then I remember the note...

"Can you... is there somewhere I can go to be in private?" I ask.

"Yeah. Follow me."

She leads me to a small room with a couple of cots and a table. "This is where the doctors and nurses sleep when we work long shifts," she explains. "Lock it behind you, and make sure you close it when you leave."

"Thank you."

I lock the door behind her and then sit on the cot, pulling the note out with my name scrawled across the front.

Dear Gage,

Let me first start by saying how much I love you. If you're reading this, it's because I'm gone, and for that, I'm sorry. They say suicide is a selfish act, and I never understood that, until now, because even as I write this letter to you, the only guilt I feel about ending my life is that I'm hurting you. You're not only my boyfriend, but my best friend, which is why it's so hard to write this letter. There are some things you need to know. But before I tell you, I need you to promise that you won't tell anyone. I'm only telling you, so you understand that my taking my life isn't because of you. If anything, the only reason I didn't do it sooner was because of you. Because of how much I love you. Every time I imagined my future, it was with you. All I ever wanted was to create a life with you. I thought I could be strong, but I'm not. I'm weak.

What I'm about to tell you, needs to stay between you and me. Once you're done reading this letter, I want you to burn it. Then get on a plane and go to LA and become the best damn drummer the music industry has ever seen. Promise me, please. Do this for me. Nothing will bring me back, and I don't want you to ruin your life because of him.

Glen. For the past several months, he's been coming into the pool house when you're not here and raping me. I know what you're thinking. Why didn't I tell you? For a couple of reasons. One, I was scared of what you'd do. I know how much you love me and would do anything to protect me, and I couldn't put you in that position. So instead, I went to my mom. I thought she would believe me and protect me like a mom is supposed to, but instead, she said that I'm sick and need help. And then I heard them talking. You went to them and begged them to help me. God, I love you for that, but there's no helping me because they don't want to help me. They want me gone. Glen is planning to run for mayor, and he sees me as a loose string. He's planning to send me away and if you stand in his way, he's going to ruin you. He's rich and has connections, and I can't let him ruin you like he's ruined me.

There's something else you need to know. I'm pregnant. I don't know how far along I am, but there's a chance it's Glen's. He caught me taking a test and told me he's going to take the baby away from me. I can't let him *do that, Gage. I'd rather die than let him take anything else away from me. I don't expect you to understand, but please know that I'm sorry and I love you. You're the best person I know, and you deserve to be happy, to have the family you never had, and I'm so sorry I couldn't be the one to give it to you.*

Be amazing.

Xo Tori

I shake myself from the past, refusing to let it take me under, and continue to soothe my daughter the best I can.

When the paramedics arrive, they take Rory from me, needing to assess her.

"Dada!" she yells, trying to reach for me. "Dada!" As her tear-filled eyes beg me to fix this, I pull out my phone, dialing the only person in the world who will make this better. The person I need by my side.

Sadie… I need Sadie.

Twenty-Nine
Sadie

I'M LOST IN THE WORDS OF A COZY MURDER MYSTERY WHEN MY PHONE RINGS, GAGE'S name coming up on the screen.

"Hey, you. How—"

"Sadie, I need you." The way he says my name, the pleading in his tone causes my body to go cold. Something's wrong. Very wrong. "It's Rory," he adds, and it's then I hear my baby girl screaming in the background. My heart clenches in my chest, feeling as though a barbed wire is wrapping around it, causing the organ to bleed out. "We're on the way to the hospital."

The hospital. They're on their way to the hospital. The recollection of Janice telling me that my husband and son were brought to the hospital but didn't make it flashed before my eyes. Collin's lifeless body, surrounded by his favorite toys he'd never play with again, being lowered into the ground.

"Gage," I gasp, the rest of my words getting caught in my throat.

"I'm so sorry, Sadie," he says, his words laced with raw emotion. "I need you to come to the hospital, please."

"Tell me she's going to be okay," I beg, sliding on my flip-flops and running out the door.

"She's hurt, but she's okay," he says. "I'm so sorry. I fucked up."

"Which hospital?"

He asks someone and then says, "New York Medical." My stomach drops. That's the same hospital Collin and Vincent were taken to. Surely, God wouldn't do this to me twice, right?

"I'm on my way."

Twenty minutes later, I'm running through the front doors of the hospital and straight to the desk. "I'm the mother of Aurora Sharp. She's been brought in by ambulance."

The nurse clicks away on the computer. "She's in the pediatric unit, room 157. Follow the animal prints on the floor, and it will take you straight there."

I do as she says, and a few minutes later, I barge into the room, where I find Gage holding a sobbing Rory.

Her eyes meet mine, and she cries harder. "Mama, ow, ow."

"Oh, thank God," I breathe, seeing that she's alive. "I'm here, sweet girl," I tell her, cutting across the room, over to her and Gage.

"I'm so sorry," Gage whispers, carefully handing me my baby. "Try not to move her arm. They think it's broken." His glassy eyes meet mine, and tears slide down his face. "I'm so damn sorry. I should've been there. I should've caught her." He shakes his head, his words making no sense.

"What happened?" I ask, cradling Rory in my arms and checking her out. Her left arm is swollen and in a tiny sling.

"She was going down the slide. Every time, I would wait until she sat down, and then I'd go to the bottom to catch her. She must've stood back up and gone to the edge. I was at the bottom when I heard her scream." Gage flinches, and fresh tears spill down his cheeks. "She fell off the side." He hangs his head, shaking it back and forth. "They think her arm is broken. They gave her medicine for pain, said it should be enough so she's not hurting, and they're preparing to have an X-ray done."

"Gage, it's okay," I tell him, reaching out and squeezing his forearm. "These things happen."

"She could've hit her head," he rasps. "Could've broken her neck. You trusted me to take care of her, and I failed you. I failed her." He steps away from us, giving us his back. "I failed my mom and Tori and our baby… And now this. Rory could've fucking died." He turns around, his features etched in pain, and my heart aches for him.

"What do you mean, Tori and your baby?" I ask. I know about Tori and his mom, but he's never mentioned a baby.

"When she killed herself, she was pregnant. I had no idea until the nurse came and told me."

"Oh, Gage." I walk over to him with Rory still sobbing in my arms. "Why didn't you tell me?"

"I was afraid," he admits softly. "I was afraid if I told you that I couldn't keep Tori's baby safe, you'd think I couldn't keep Rory safe. You've already lost two babies." He swallows thickly, his sad blue eyes locking with mine. "Looks like it ended up happening anyway. Maybe if I'd told you, this could've been prevented."

"Don't you dare go there," I say, refusing to let him do this to himself. "That is not the same thing. You were not responsible for your mom's death or for keeping Tori and her baby safe. There's nothing you could've done to protect or save them." I reach out and lay my palm on the side of his tearstained cheek. "You can't let that guilt weigh on your shoulders. It wasn't your fault, just like Rory getting hurt wasn't your fault. It's part of being a parent. Every day, all we can do is love our babies and pray they're safe. But at any moment, they can be taken from us."

I lean over and kiss Rory's forehead, and she sighs softly, her eyes fluttering closed, the pain meds and exhaustion making her sleepy. "Yes, she got hurt. But it could've happened with me or anyone watching her. Life is unpredictable. You can't keep shouldering the responsibility and blame."

I sit on the chair and pat the one next to me, and Gage joins me. "Were you clean and sober?"

"Of course," he chokes out.

"Were you watching her?"

"Yeah, but—"

"It was an accident. She broke her arm, and that sucks, but it was just that… an accident."

"She was in so much pain."

"Did you take care of her?" I ask, already knowing the answer but needing him to hear it. "Did you hold her in the ambulance and make sure she knew she was safe?"

He nods, tears pricking his eyes. "I was so scared, Sadie. I had a flashback from when Tori died, and I was scared it was going to take me under."

"So what did you do?"

"I called you," he chokes out. "I'm so sorry," he sobs. "If you don't want me to take her—"

"Nope," I say, pressing my fingers to his lips, refusing to let him finish that thought. "I don't trust you any less with her than I did before the accident. You did everything you could." I lean over and kiss his wet lips. "I love you, Gage."

We sit in silence for several minutes, and then the technician comes in, bringing an X-ray machine with her. She takes pictures of Rory's arm and then the doctor confirms that it's broken. After realigning the bone, a bright pink cast is put on her arm—her choice—and then we're discharged with a prescription for meds and a referral to see the pediatric orthopedic doctor in four weeks.

Gage remains quiet when we get home, holding Rory and lying with her while she falls asleep. I give him his space, reading a book since I can't focus enough to work.

Once she's asleep, he comes out and sits next to me, lifting my legs into his lap. "Thank you for being there," he says, massaging my feet.

"We're partners," I tell him. "When you need me, I'll be here, just like when I need you, I know you'll be here too." He squeezes my foot and smiles softly at me.

We sit in comfortable silence, both of us lost in our thoughts. I don't know why, but the song he wrote for me plays in my head, and I sigh, thinking about how true the lyrics are.

"For what it's worth…" I sit up and climb onto his lap. "You healed me. My heart was broken and bleeding, and you fixed it by giving me the greatest gift… our daughter." His eyes light up in understanding. "It's because of her, because of *you,* I'm finally living again."

He wraps his arms around me, and I kiss him tenderly on his lips, then nestle my head into the crook of his neck, enjoying the comfort of being held by Gage.

"There's something I need to do, and it'd mean a lot if you'd join me," he says after a few minutes. "Do you think you could ask Janice to come over and watch Rory? We won't be long."

"TORI, I'D LIKE YOU TO MEET SADIE. I WANTED YOU TO MEET HER BECAUSE SHE AND RORY, our beautiful daughter, wouldn't be here if it weren't for you." Gage sniffles, and I wrap my arms around him, holding him tight.

"I hate that you're gone," he says, "but something good, something bright came from the darkness of your death. I met Sadie."

He pulls a crumpled paper out of his pocket and opens it up. "It took me a while to do as you asked, but I've finally done it." He glances at me, a small smile playing on his lips. "I've found happiness." He pulls a lighter out of his pocket and sets the corner of the paper on fire, dropping it onto the stone of her grave.

"She asked me to burn the letter after I read it," he explains. "I held on to it, reading it over and over again, wanting to remind myself of how badly I failed." He places his hand in mine. "I think it's time to move on. To let go of the past and focus on our present… on our future."

Epilogue

Sadie

SIX MONTHS LATER

"THANK YOU, NEW YORK, AND HAPPY NEW YEAR!" CAMDEN YELLS AS THE CROWD SCREAMS in excitement. It's New Year's Eve, and Raging Chaos just finished their performance in Times Square. It's freezing cold outside, but there was no way I was missing their performance. Rory is at home with Janice and Henry, warm and toasty and fast asleep. Gage made plans for us to stay at a hotel overnight to ring in the new year once their show is over.

"One more thing," Gage says, shocking the hell out of me and everyone else. He plays the drums. He doesn't sing… or talk. "Sadie, can you come out here, please?"

It takes me a second to wrap my head around what he's asking, but when he smiles my way and nods, I put one foot in front of the other to join him on stage.

"What are you doing?" I whisper-yell.

"This is my girlfriend," he says to the crowd, making them cheer.

"Hi." I wave my hand quickly.

"I've thought about how to do this a million times, but every time it feels like it's not romantic enough, or the timing isn't right," he says. "So I figured tonight would be perfect. What better way to start the new year than with you as my fiancée?" He quirks a brow. "Shoot, I probably should've proposed first. And now that I'm thinking about it, if you say no, it's going to be a crappy way to start the year."

The crowd bursts out in laughter at Gage's botched proposal, and I join in, shaking my head. "Well, there's only one way to know if it will be a good or bad year," I say, only realizing too late that because of the mic on him, everyone can hear me.

"Oh, yeah." He fumbles with his pocket and then pulls out a black box, popping it open. "Since the day I met you, I knew you were a game changer. You're the lightness in my dark, the healer to my broken. You remind me every day that life is worth living, so I would love nothing more than to spend my life with you as my wife."

Gage drops to his knee and holds out the ring. "Sadie Ruiz, will you do me the honor of becoming my wife?"

"Umm…" I lift my finger to my chin and tap it playfully, and Gage chuckles. "Yes, I would love to be your wife."

A massive grin stretches across his face as he pushes the ring onto my finger and then stands, lifting me in his arms and twirling me around.

"It's probably for the best anyway," I whisper, so only he can hear. "We already have one child out of wedlock. Maybe this baby will be born with his or her parents married."

Gage stiffens at my half-joke and releases me, his blue eyes locking with my green. "Are you…?" He looks down at my still flat belly. I only just found out this morning. I planned to tell him once we were alone tonight after the show.

"I am… We are." I smile a watery smile, and he pulls me into his arms, hugging me tightly.

"Fuck, baby," he murmurs into my ear. "Thank you."

"Do we have time to stop at Eternal Cross on the way to the hotel?" I ask as we make our way off the stage. "I'd like to tell Collin he's going to be a big brother again."

Gage nods and tugs me into his side, kissing my temple. "We have all the time in the world."

Want more of Sadie and Gage?
Find some sexy and sweet bonus scenes on my website.

Did you know Camden, Braxton,
and Declan also have books?
Check out the other books in the *Love & Lyrics Series*:

Did you know Camden's parents have their own book?
Check out *A Chance Encounter*.

About the Author

Reading is like breathing in, writing is like breathing out.
— Pam Allyn

Nikki Ash resides in South Florida where she is an English teacher by day and a writer by night. When she's not writing, you can find her with a book in her hand. From the Boxcar Children, to Wuthering Heights, to the latest single parent romance, she has lived and breathed every type of book. While reading and writing are her passions, her two children are her entire world. You can probably find them at a Disney park before you would find them at home on the weekends!

e5ef69ba-ab25-404e-b865-b999d10c6090R01